DARK MOOR GUARDIANS

A KISS OF STONE
DARK MOOR GUARDIANS

BRENNA ASH

He needed to remind himself he was *only* there to *protect* her...

By day, Gregor Magnuson is a bodyguard to the stars, responsible for keeping Hollywood's elite safe. By night, when he's not defending the mortal world, he's tasked with capturing wayward demons and returning them to the otherworld where they belong. This gargoyle-human hybrid is part of an elite warrior guard, the Dark Moor Guardians. After letting his heart get in the way of a previous job that ended in disaster, Gregor swore he'd never make the same mistake again.

Krista Wallingford is Hollywood's reigning scream queen and a hopeless romantic, who has no idea Supernaturals exist. When a rogue skin walker becomes obsessed with her, Gregor is hired as her new security detail. Krista has a long history of getting involved with the wrong guy and the relationships never end well. She suspects Gregor is one of those guys. Yet, she can't deny the magnetic pull she feels the instant she lays eyes on her new bodyguard.

Gregor feels that pull as well, and he soon finds himself wanting to protect Krista for more than the lucrative money he'll be paid. Could she become part of his world or will her newfound knowledge of a supernatural world be too much to take?

A Kiss of Stone
Brenna Ash

Copyright © 2019 by Brenna Ash
Dark Moor Media, LLC

Cover Design: Wicked Smart Designs

ISBN: 978-1-7330367-0-2

ACKNOWLEDGMENTS

This book was a long time in the making. There are so many people to thank and I'm sure I'll miss someone, but believe me it was completely unintentional.

To my editor, Bethany Oliver, you've helped me bring Gregor and Krista's story to life and didn't kill me in the process. Thank you!! I promise I'll watch those commas next time.

STAR and the Rocket Girls, you know who you are. You ladies rock!

A special shout out to Chris K. Thank you so much! You rock!

My travel buddies, Andrea and Eliza. I look forward to all the research trips in our future.

And of course, my family. I couldn't do this without all your support.

The Legend of the Dark Moor Guardians

There are those that say the supernatural doesn't exist. Those who only believe what they can touch, see and feel. Whether it's their belief system, their religion or their upbringing, the thought of supernatural beings walking among the living is implausible.

These non-believers live in their own closed world, refusing to acknowledge that there are more than humans out there walking the earth amongst them.

It's because of these non-believers that the Superior Council was created. To keep the mortal world a safe haven for humans to walk without fear of the unknown.

The council consists of nine board members, representing a wide range of otherworldly beings. Each member was chosen because of how high they rank within their own supernatural line. A witch, a vampire, a werewolf, a shifter, a fairy, a ghost, a goddess, a demon, and a succubus. Though often at odds with one another, these leaders have learned to work together to keep the human world blissfully ignorant.

These nine beings were tasked with devising a plan to keep the mortals safe and in denial. To protect the separation between mortals and supernaturals.

Retirement communities were built to house those beings that were unable to live peacefully among the humans. If an immortal was caught wreaking havoc, they were captured and sent to one of these communities. As part of their 'retirement', each tenant is forced to sign a contract giving up their disruptive ways. Once signed, they're not allowed to cross over into the mortal world ever again.

But eternity is a very long time and supernaturals are

restless beings. It's hard to keep them in check, adhering to rules when they never had to before.

With this knowledge, the Superior Council knew they needed an army. A group of elite warriors they could dispatch at any time to return the rogue beings back to the Otherworld and the Council for trial and sentencing.

The Dark Moor Guardians are those warriors. They live in the mortal world. Blending into society. But are ready to answer the call whenever they are summoned. The Guardians originated in the moors of northern Scotland. The first faction was founded there. And though there are others in locations throughout the world, they all carry the same name.

These are the Dark Moor Guardians.

CHAPTER ONE

The Kingdom of The Superior Council was invisible to the naked eye. One had to know it was there to see it. The invisibility cloak shrouded the compound within a mass of trees. Anyone walking by would just see a thick forest. It amazed Gregor Magnuson how dismissive humans were when it came to the supernatural. He'd been dealing with them for so many years and no one that he'd ever come across knew anything of his world. They didn't believe it existed.

He stood in front of the main building, as the complex slowly revealed itself to him as he waited for the gates to swing open and allow him in.

After being summoned year after year, he shouldn't be nervous. The Council had a way of getting under his skin. It pissed him off. The sooner he was given his assignment and could leave, the better.

The phone call summoning him to the Kingdom came in a few hours ago. In the middle of a workout.

"Magnuson. Three O'clock sharp." That's all they said before they hung up.

The order had him pounding the shit out of a punching bag suspended from the ceiling. The rattle of the chains a welcome noise as the bag swayed away from him with each punch. He imagined each one of The Superiors taking the full force of each hit.

Elitist bastards. The expectation was that he would drop everything and appear as demanded.

With every determined step he took and each echo of his boots off the shiny black marble floors of the Great hall, his movements stiffened. He used a handkerchief to wipe his sweaty palms, and shoved it back in his pocket. Why did he always feel like a condemned man being led to his death when he was summoned to appear? The Superiors needed him. Without him and the other Guardians dispatched throughout the mortal world, they'd never get their rogue demons back. Outside of his sister, Rona, he would have a hard time naming the others. Each Guardian covered a specific area. He'd been tasked with America some decades ago, and had moved around from state to state.

Eventually, he'd love to go back home to Scotland and work. But unless Rona decided to resign, he was out of luck. And resignation wasn't an option. The job of a Dark Moor Guardian was a lifetime assignment. Usually until death.

As if on cue, his sister walked toward him. "Rona?"

"Gregor!" She ran to him and he scooped her up in a warm hug. "I didn't know ye'd be here today." Her strong brogue had him longing for home even more.

Setting her on her feet, he took a step back. "Me either. I just got the call this afternoon." She nodded, her red curls bouncing. It'd been years since he'd seen his sister. "How are you? Things at home okay?"

"We're good. We miss ye." She said quietly, knowing it was a touchy subject. Her golden eyes took him in. "The states look like they've been good to ye." She smiled, but he noted the sadness in her eyes.

This wasn't a conversation he wanted to have. Not here. Not now. "Well, I have to get inside," he dipped his head toward the end of the hall. "Mustn't keep the bosses waiting."

Rona stepped forward and embraced him once more. "Come home when ye get a chance. We'd love a visit."

Nodding curtly, he refused to voice a promise he would only break later, and then turned, back stiff and straight, and continued down the hall.

He looked up at the massive columns that lined the creamy white walls, and then at the guards standing beside each one. What was their purpose? To take him out if he didn't obey the Superiors? They didn't say a word as he made his way toward the thick, solid white oak doors that would lead him to The Superior Council.

Two attendants bowed as he neared, then pulled the huge doors open, allowing him entrance into a room he'd become all too familiar with.

He paused before an intricately carved table set on the far side of the room. The symbols etched into the wood represented languages lost to time. He dipped low, as was the custom when greeting those responsible for keeping balance between the two worlds. He hated the old traditions. Didn't see the need for them in today's modern world.

He lived on earth, walked among mostly mortals, and loved it. Especially, the freedom from all the restrictions of the old world.

"Thank you for coming," the Vampire Superior said, her Slavic accent strong. *Like he had a choice.* "We have someone we need you to return to our world. You'll be compensated well."

Gregor waited for more information. He knew this song and dance well. It did him no good to ask questions.

He didn't know their names. Only knew the supernatural family they represented.

The Witch Superior produced a folder and held it out to him. Stepping forward, he accepted the manila envelope from her old bony, wrinkled hands. "Thaddeus has journeyed to Moon Bay, Florida. Since you're familiar with the city, we're assigning him to you. Everything you need to know is in this file." The council members looked at each other before focusing their attention back on Gregor.

His pulse quickened at the name. Could it be?

"Dismissed."

"That's it? That's all you're going to tell me?"

"Silence!" The Goddess Superior demanded.

"You're sending me after Thaddeus. If you expect me to hand him over in one piece, you should really rethink that."

With a final, sarcastic bow, he turned and walked out of the Council Room and back through the Great Hall, only pausing once he was outside. His adrenaline running high. Just once, he'd like to tell them what he thought of their holier-than-thou attitudes, but he enjoyed his head and would like to keep it. He walked through the gates and joined the mortal world again. To anyone that happened to pass by at that time, they'd think Gregor had taken a stroll in the woods.

He hadn't been to Moon Bay since the eighties, when he dated a woman there. Nothing but big hair and bad memories lived there for him. If luck was on his side, Tiffany Parker would have moved far away from the tiny, but bustling, coastal city.

The last time he'd seen her, she was throwing his belongings onto the front lawn of the apartment complex where they were living together. The woman was convinced that he was having an affair with the bartender at the club where he was working as a bouncer.

He wasn't and he was pissed off that she had thought so. But, later, he realized he'd dodged a bullet. That one was crazy with a capital C.

He hadn't been back since. It was also the last time he'd seen his older brother., Gunther, who was Chief of police at the Moon Bay Police Department now. The Magnuson's weren't a close family. Gatherings during the holidays weren't a family tradition.

In his car, he opened the envelope and scanned the contents.

"You've got to be fucking kidding me," he yelled inside the empty cabin. *Thaddeus.* The name played like acid on Gregor's tongue. He'd dealt with the skin walker before. He had unfinished business with him.

After all, he was one of the reasons Katherine was no longer here.

THE CAMERAS FLASHED, their bright lights blinding her. This was something she would never get used to. Oh, and the hordes of people, too. Grabbing at her, throwing questions her way. There was never any privacy, let alone peace. Some days she wondered if it was all worth it. Today was one of those days. But, like always, she plastered a smile on her face and willingly ventured into the shark tank.

"Krista," the reporter shouted, "with all the paranormal movies you've starred in over the years, what are your thoughts on the supernatural? Are you a believer?"

Inside, Krista Wallingford wanted to scream. Something she was good at being the reigning Scream Queen of Hollywood. This was a question she had to answer in every interview. Why it annoyed her so much she really couldn't say. It just did. Maybe she was being irrational. Did people really believe that because you play a part in a movie that's who you are in real life? Are they that stupid? She wanted to scream at them. *I'm acting!* But, she couldn't do that, so, she smiled and gave a half-hearted chuckle. "No, I'm a non-believer. I've never seen anything to show me otherwise."

"Are you saying you want someone to provide you with proof?" The question was asked by an interviewer who was skinny with straight black hair, and round glasses who didn't look old enough to drive. He reminded her of a popular and beloved bespectacled children's character.

"Absolutely not. I'm just saying nothing has ever presented itself." She twisted the cap off the bottle of water placed in front of her on the cloth-covered table and gave the side eye to her publicist to move the questions along. These interviews were her least favorite part of the job. Give her a script to read and memorize. Put her in a dressing room for wardrobe decisions. Hell, put her in a makeup chair for hours on end while they create a whole new look for her. She'd take any of those over these dreaded media blitzes.

"Have you signed on for the next installment in the series?"

"Nothing's set in stone but talks between my team and production are ongoing."

"Can you expand on that?"

"Not at this time." Krista said, then pushed back her chair, the legs scraping loudly on the staging floor and stood. She was done. Whether they were or not.

Taking that as her cue, her publicist, Natalie stepped up to the mic as everyone started yelling their questions all at once, trying to get one more morsel they could report on.

"Thank you all for coming. That concludes this interview session." She picked up Krista's water bottle and walked off the stage, following her biggest client to a seating area near a large window overlooking the city.

"That was a tough one."

"I'm so tired of these press conferences. I feel like I'm constantly pimping myself out." She sighed. "What's next on our list?"

"That's it for today. We need to talk about your next project."

Krista was exhausted. The only thing she wanted to do was soak in a nice, hot bubble bath and enjoy a bottle of wine.

"Can we discuss it tomorrow. I just want to be done for the day."

Natalie had a distressed look on her face. The young woman wanted to work twenty-four seven and she wasn't ready yet to call it a day. Krista admired her work ethic. She was Natalie's first client. She'd taken a huge risk hiring someone with no publicist experience, but when she came in for an interview, they clicked right away.

Natalie worried her lower lip, not saying anything.

Seeing the dejected look on Natalie's face made her feel awful. "I'm sorry. I'm just tired and it's making me cranky."

"I understand. Is there anything else that you need for today?"

"No, thank you, though. How about we talk in the morning. Say, 10:30?" She asked, trying to lessen the blow.

"Okay." Natalie said, her whole face brightening. "I'll bring the car around to take you home."

Home was a two-story, five-bedroom, six-bath spread deep in the Hollywood foothills with an eight-foot stone fence surrounding her property. It was still part of the city, but far enough out that no crazy fans or media bothered her.

She snagged a bottle of Merlot out of the wine cooler and dug around in the utility drawer for the corkscrew, tempted to forgo the glass. Her eyes touched upon the thick stack of mail on the white granite countertop. She wasn't in the mood to deal with that now.

Glass of wine in hand, she made her way to the bathroom. She'd ditched her shoes at the front door and now the tile was cool on her feet.

Ten minutes later, she was up to her shoulders in bubbles and hot water. Her favorite top-40 station blaring from the speakers set into the walls of the room. The whole house had surround sound. One of the best investments she'd ever made.

The script of her next movie was on the bath shelf, next to the bottle of wine, tempting her to read it, but she just wanted to lay back, sip her wine and let the stress of the day slowly ease out of her tired limbs.

She closed her eyes and let the rhythm of the music sweep her away.

The wine was going down easy when her favorite song came on. She moved in sync with the music, ignoring the water that splashed over the sides of the claw-foot tub. She'd wipe it up later.

And then she screamed for real as the sound of shattering glass and her security system started blaring. Scaring the ever-loving shit out of her.

CHAPTER TWO

Watching in anger at the press conference earlier, Thaddeus felt his blood boil as Krista voiced her denial about spirits and the unexplained. Wanting nothing more than to show her the darker side of life that she refused to see. A whole world existed out there. She'd be able to see it all if she just opened her mind. Enjoy it for what it was. What it stood for.

The things he could show her. Incredible things. She'd been his obsession for a long time. He'd been watching her, hoping she'd see the light. He was tired of waiting. So, when the chance presented itself, he moved.

Entering the mortal world exhilarated him. It'd been so long since he'd been here.

There was no mistaking that Hillsview was beautiful, even peaceful. Retirement was all fun and games, but, boring as fuck. He couldn't take any more ice cream socials. Needed some excitement that wasn't scheduled. A day that wasn't planned out for him and the other residents. If he had to play one more damn game of shuffleboard with Jericho, he was going to off himself.

His time on this side was limited. He knew the Superior Council was aware he'd left the second he stepped into the mortal world. No doubt, a Guardian already dispatched to hunt him down and bring him home. He wasn't supposed to be here. None of them were. At least not after they'd retired. Once they hit that retirement button, they had to sign on the dotted line saying they'd play nice and stay away from the land of the living. Sounded fine at first.

But, when you're immortal, eternity is a long time to behave, and just sitting around made things worse. Pining for the glory days when you could get away with causing a raucous. He missed that.

He had to move quickly to put his plan in place. If the Guardian caught him, he'd never enjoy any type of freedom again. Eternity spent in the equivalent of solitary confinement did not appeal to him.

A lot of his time was spent watching television. Movies. Horror was his favorite. Especially paranormal flicks tailored to make the audience scream. That's where Thaddeus first laid eyes on Krista Wallingford.

Every night he passed the hours away binge-watching anything the starlet had ever appeared in. He obsessed over every word that escaped her full, pouty lips. Then he found out she didn't believe beings like him existed. Humans were so oblivious to what was right in front of them. He'd make her see. Make her open her eyes to all that's she's been missing.

Now, watching her bathe, his pulse quickened, the pull to make contact with Krista was strong. Oh, how he wanted to feel her soft skin under his calloused hands.

Her house was locked up tight. If he really wanted to, he could probably make it past security. But he found the unknown to be more frightening.

He looked around the outer perimeter of the house,

zoning in on a large rock. Perfect. He walked to the side of the house, scoping out the windows and chose one near the back, and tossed the rock straight through it, causing glass to shatter everywhere.

Her scream made him smile. He slinked back into the bushes, watching the time to see how long it took for the authorities to arrive.

IN HIS GARGOYLE FORM, Gregor watched as police secured the perimeter of Krista's house. Officers with flashlights illuminated the yard as they searched for the perpetrator. He was certain they wouldn't find anyone.

This was Thaddeus's calling card. His scent was just a faint whisper in the wind. The skin walker was either long gone or had taken the face and body of one of the local policemen. If that was the case, Gregor couldn't differentiate him from the real officer unless he did something to alert him. Which wasn't likely.

At this point, Gregor doubted the skin walker would risk getting caught. Because if he really was after Krista, he wouldn't chance giving up the game now.

So then, why throw a rock through her window? It didn't make any sense. To gain her attention? To scare her? It just wasn't adding up. There had to be something more to it. A deeper motive than just trying to scare her. It was such a juvenile move.

Two officers stopped to talk right near where Gregor was, and paid no attention to him. One of the many perks of being able to turn yourself to stone on a whim. A side effect of being a hybrid. Unlike his father, who turned to stone as soon as the sun came up, Gregor and his siblings were able to turn to stone by choice.

He listened to the officer's conversation, but they didn't say anything he didn't already know.

After a few minutes they moved on, leaving Gregor to silently keep watch.

And hours later, after the police were long gone, he still sat in that same spot, waiting and watching.

Thaddeus hadn't made an appearance. Knowing he had to pick Krista up at the airport in the morning, Gregor changed into his human form and gave the house a once-over.

A sudden urge to enter the house overcame him. The need to go inside strong. He'd never met the woman, but he felt a strange pull to learn more about her.

Not wanting to invade the starlet's privacy, he hopped the fence and walked away from the house before calling an Uber to pick him up and take him to the airport.

Krista was safe. Tucked away at her agent's house for the evening so there was no need for him to hang around. Plus, he needed to beat her to Moon Bay.

NERVOUS AND SHAKEN UP, Krista paced the floor of her agent's penthouse, the tile cool on her bare feet. There was no way Jessica Burke was going to allow Krista to go back home and insisted she stay with her while the broken window at her house was repaired. And Krista was relieved. The last place she wanted to be right now, was home alone.

The police thought it was nothing more than a group of kids with nothing better to do who had thrown the rock through her window, and while Krista wasn't sure if that were true, Jessica thought there was more to it. Either way, it scared the ever-loving Hell out of her.

And right now she was done talking about it.

So, instead they discussed her upcoming movie.

Krista took a deep breath and sighed. "I don't want to go to Florida. It's the middle of July. Do you know how dreadfully hot and humid it's going to be there?"

She made a mental note to know exactly where her next movie would be shot before she ever signed another damn contract, because right now she was really regretting that decision. Florida. She hated it in July.

"Krista." Her agent sighed. "You need to do this for two reasons. Moon Bay is the setting of your next movie and it's far enough away from L.A. that your stalker, whoever the hell it is, will leave you alone."

"We have no idea if I really have a stalker." Krista sighed loudly. "Remember, the police said it was just a bunch of kids fooling around. She collapsed on the overstuffed couch and hugged a navy pillow. "I don't want to go to Florida. Do you know what that heat will do to my hair?"

"There is more to it than just a broken window, Krista. And anyway, you have a stylist. They'll take care of your hair. Stop being so dramatic." Jessica said shaking her head. "And besides, we've requested the protection of a very well-known bodyguard."

"Fine!" Krista coalesced. "But only because the production company is paying me big bucks for this film."

"That's the attitude I want to see." Jessica was all business. Even in the comfort of her own home late at night, the woman was dressed in a sharp pant suit, her brown hair pulled back into a severe bun.

Krista stuck out her tongue, "Whatever. So, who's this famous bodyguard?"

Jessica rolled her eyes. "Someone that's worked a lot of dangerous, high-profile cases."

"In Hollywood?"

"Yes. Remember when Amy Ryan couldn't even step out

of her house or even answer her door? This is the guy that took him down. He's good, Krista."

Krista shrugged. She knew when she was on the losing end of an argument. With a sigh, she asked, "When do I leave?"

"You're booked on the red-eye for tomorrow night. Gregor Magnuson will pick you up at the airport." Jessica handed her the itinerary with her flight information. "Just a forewarning. He's hot. Remember, he's there to protect you, not entertain you."

Krista scoffed. "Please! Like I would ever fall for a bodyguard."

Jessica snorted. "Like you ever wouldn't."

CHAPTER THREE

I nside the Orlando airport, Gregor scanned the hordes of passengers descending the stairs making their way to grab their luggage, looking for Krista Wallingford and keeping an eye out for anyone that may be around her acting suspicious.

The possibility of Thaddeus blending in with the crowd, his face could be anyone, had him on edge.

The second Gregor laid eyes on Krista, he felt the weight of her energy as he spotted her in baggage claim. He'd watched a few of her movies, so he could learn a little bit about her, but the screen didn't do her justice. Her presence demanded attention by her just being there.

She was gorgeous, flawless, with a body made for sin. He refused to focus on that right now, or on her, not in that way. Ever since Katherine he'd kept his record clean by never getting involved with a client again. He didn't plan to break that streak now, no matter how sexy she was.

And with Thaddeus being the one stalking Krista? The comparison and what the possible outcome could be wasn't lost on Gregor.

Nothing good ever came from mixing business with pleasure. It was like friends and money. You never confused the two. If you did, you just opened yourself up to heartbreak.

And death.

But as he approached her, ready to introduce himself, their eyes met and she locked those big brown eyes onto him. She was going to make this job difficult.

Very difficult.

Damn.

THE SECOND she stepped off the plane the cloying heat, heavy with humidity took Krista's breath away. She was sweating bullets by the time she walked into the airport. A direct contrast to the dry heat of California she was used to. She slipped on her sunglasses and straw hat and made her way to baggage claim, looking like every other tourist excited to start their vacation in the Sunshine State. Except she wasn't excited. Miserable was more like it. The heat was making her irritable and thirsty.

An iced latte would be perfect right now. But she didn't want to hang around the airport any longer than she had to. The sooner she got settled in the better. She'd just have to ask her driver stop at a coffee shop on the way to the hotel. There was bound to be one on the way.

While she stood at the luggage carousel, and watched the suitcases go around and around with boredom, she took off her sunglasses and plopped them on the brim of the hat, and scanned the people waiting. She didn't recognize anyone, not that she expected to. And no one seemed to notice her, either. Jessica was overreacting about the whole stalker thing. It was probably some jerk looking for a thrill who had way too much time on his hands.

Creepy guys came with the territory. This wasn't her first time dealing with one. She'd had some weird shit mailed to her, but again, she didn't think it was anything to be worried about. At one point in their career, every actor received some odd stuff. Whoever it was this time, she didn't think he'd ever harm her or show up on her doorstep. He hadn't yet, and if the police were right about it being a bunch of bored kids that broke her window, why would she think he'd follow her across the country? Chances are, he wouldn't. But, Jessica thought otherwise, so she'd have to deal with having a body-guard with her at all times. It was a small price to pay. Though if she did have a stalker who was to say it was just one? Maybe she had a bunch of shitty fans.

It wasn't a far stretch to think there might be multiple weirdos out there considering the type of movies she worked on. The crazies were strong.

She looked around a little more, still waiting to grab her luggage and spotted Gregor Magnuson right away. His stride was purposeful as he made his way through the crowd toward her. She watched people just move out of his way, as if a silent cue told them to steer clear or face the conse-quences. She slipped the mirrored sunglasses back on and studied him thankful for the discreetness they offered as she tracked his approach. Damn. He was huge. Bigger than her usual security detail. And he never took his eyes off her.

If she hadn't been wearing sunglasses his gaze would have made her uncomfortable, and even worse, she'd be embar-rassed because she couldn't take her eyes off him either. He was tall, with light golden hair, and ice blue eyes that looked like they could freeze you on the spot. A shiver worked its way through her body. Jessica wasn't lying when she'd told Krista to beware. He was going to be dangerous. In more ways than one.

She sighed as she waited for him to close the distance

between them. Gregor Magnuson was akin to a beautiful Nordic God. All hard planes and tanned skin. It was going to be really hard to keep her hands to herself if they were going to be in such close proximity during her time in Moon Bay.

He stopped, towering over her as he held out his hand for her to shake.

"Miss Wallingford. I'm Gregor." He gave her a stiff nod. "Nice to meet you." His body language screamed business.

His voice held a slight accent, like he wasn't from the states, but she couldn't quite place it. And for once in her life, she found herself speechless as his strong hand enveloped hers.

"How many bags do you have?"

"Three." She managed to say.

He raised a pale eyebrow in question.

"Don't judge me. I'm going to be here for a while." She snapped, pulling herself together.

He lifted his hands in defense. Huge, strong hands, she noted, with long fingers. "No judgment here. I'm just glad I rented an SUV."

Krista put her hand up, tiny in comparison to his. "Hold on. You're driving?" Where was her driver? A truck? She didn't want to be riding around in a truck.

"I am. I've got a license and everything." The corner of his mouth lifted up in a smirk, making his eyes twinkle.

"I don't need you to drive me. I have a driver."

"You sure do." He winked. "Yours truly."

"But..."

He was making her lose her train of thought. She could barely string a coherent sentence together. No one ever did that to her. She was always in control. But she wasn't right now.

"But nothing," he said, smiling at her, a wicked gleam in

his eyes. "It's all been arranged. I'm here to protect you and I can't do that if you're not with me."

She kept concentrating on his lips. Soft, full lips. She wondered what they would feel like kissing her neck. Damn, it was worse than she thought.

"That's not really necessary."

"Oh, but it is. Anyway, it's my job. So just wait here while I get your luggage."

She wanted to throw a smart-ass remark back at him, but all she could do was nod.

So, while they waited, she took the time to study him. His eyes were amazing, almost unworldly. They were such a pale blue they almost didn't seem human. And the gray suit he wore, she couldn't stop staring at it. At him. The man could wear a suit. It molded to his muscles in sheer perfection. There was no way it came off a rack. Not when it fit him like that. It must've been custom made.

"Oh, there's one of mine." Krista pointed to a bright purple case covered in multi-colored polka dots, coming around the belt. She wasn't ashamed to admit she admired his ass as he bent over and grabbed her bag, setting it down easily beside her. "I've got two more exactly like that."

He gave her the side-eye, which she chose to ignore. She wasn't sure how he did it, because her bags were super heavy, but he managed to get all three of them off the conveyor belt, out of the airport and into the short-term parking lot in record time while she trailed along beside him, holding on to her hat to keep it from blowing off.

"So, is there any chance I can talk you into stopping for a coffee on our way to the hotel?" She could already feel the moisture forming on her skin, the humidity heavy in the air. Now she remembered all the reasons she didn't want to be here. The exhausting heat. The hordes of people. Even the smell of suntan lotion. It was all nauseating.

"You know this isn't L.A., right?" He tossed her suitcases effortlessly in the back of a black Tahoe.

What was that supposed to mean? Of course, she knew this wasn't Los Angeles, because if it was, they wouldn't be here having this stupid conversation. She hoped the heat was just making him irritable as well. Because, right now, his attitude sucked.

"Are you saying there are no coffee shops in Florida?" Krista asked, irritation apparent in her snippety tone. She'd asked for a cup of coffee for Christ's sake, not the moon and stars.

"There are plenty."

"Then what's the problem?"

"No problem. We just don't have a Starbucks on every corner. At least not in Moon Bay." Gregor said, making sure her luggage was safely stored away in the back of the Tahoe before he pushed the hatch closed.

"It doesn't have to be a Starbucks." She said, incredulous. "Any place I can get a coffee would be great."

"What kind of coffee do you want?"

"Nothing fancy." Krista crossed her arms over her chest and stared daggers at him though he couldn't see her eyes because of her sunglasses. "Just an iced, skinny latte, two pumps vanilla, stirred, light on the ice."

"Nothing fancy, huh?"

If she didn't know any better, she'd take the look that Gregor was giving her as a combination of disbelief and confirmation. "What? You can't tell me that Moon Bay is a black-coffee-only kind of place."

"Get in," he held the passenger door open, ignoring her question, and shut it after she slid easily into the seat.

She waited as he walked around the back of the truck, opening the driver's side door and quickly settled into the cool, leather seat beside her, the SUV dipping in response to his weight. He looked over at Krista and blessed her with a small smile, causing her heart to skip a beat.

Keeping her hands to herself might be easier said than done.

THADDEUS WAITED for what felt like hours before he caught a glimpse of Krista. His excitement rose, causing butterflies to dance in his stomach. She always had that effect on him. Even when he was watching her on the small screen he had in his room at Hillview. Since he didn't know what flight she'd be on, he'd arrived at the airport early that morning and settled until she landed.

Every time a flight's arrival from LAX was announced, he perked up. Anxious to lay eyes on her.

But she was worth the wait.

He had spotted her right away. She was wearing a pair of sunglasses and a huge, floppy hat, she tried to blend in with the crowd, but her beauty couldn't be hidden that easily. One smile and anyone with half a brain could tell it was her.

Not to mention the tell-tale sway of her hips.

He couldn't wait until she was his, until they were together. Really together. For over a year, he'd been waiting for the perfect moment to introduce himself, but the timing had never panned out. Until now. He couldn't have asked for a better place. Moon Bay was the ultimate backdrop because, for one, it was out of the spotlight of the Holly-wood hills, not that it wasn't easy for someone to blend in there, but people were always around. Watching. Cameras flashing. Security hovering. This was so much better. More discreet.

He'd continued to watch as Krista approached a massive rock of a man. Her security? Had to be. The guy was a hulk.

Much bigger than he'd ever be. Most likely all brawn and no brains. And that's where he had the advantage.

He could outsmart him.

Before all brawn-no-brain knew what was happening, Krista would be gone.

He monitored them closely as her security guard moved up to the carousel, retrieved her luggage and then motioned for her to follow him out the door.

Finally. Walking at a discreet distance behind them, he stopped for a moment to toss the newspaper he'd finished reading hours ago in the trash, and to see which way they were going. The minute they headed toward the bank of elevators, he knew they were parked on one of the upper levels. Lucky for him, his rental was on the lower level. So, he hurried out of the airport, jumped into his car, then paid his parking fee in cash to make sure he didn't leave a paper trail, and then waited near the exit. There was only one way out. They'd have to pass right by him.

And just when he was beginning to think he'd somehow missed them, a black SUV exited the garage. As they drove by his suspicions were confirmed. Mr. Muscles was driving.

He followed at a safe distance, not wanting to give himself away or to cause concern. When they turned into The Breeze hotel, he slowed, but didn't follow. It was enough to know where she was staying for now. He'd contact them tomorrow and see if there were any rooms available. If not, he'd stay at one of the other nearby hotels. There weren't many in Moon Bay and with the movie filming in town, the rooms were more than likely booked, but he'd have to take a chance.

Tonight, he'd just sleep in his car, thoughts of making Krista Wallingford see the dark side of the world dancing in his dreams.

CHAPTER FOUR

I f it made any sense, the city of Moon Bay was one of those unique places that blended city life with the charm of rural beach living.

Krista watched the crowded buildings of the inner city give way to a beautiful harbor docked with everything from small dinghies to massive yachts.

She leaned against the cool window, staring out at the palm trees as they whizzed by, eventually to be replaced by mossy oaks and maple trees, and sighed. Florida really was beautiful, even if it did wreak havoc on her hair. They were quiet as he drove. Gregor was focused on the road and she was trying not to focus on him. Yes, she enjoyed the silence, the contentment.

If she were being honest, in a very selfish way, she didn't want the car ride to end. If she could have found a way to prolong it, she would have. But she couldn't think of a single thing that wouldn't clue him in to exactly what she was doing, so it wasn't long before he pulled off the two-lane road and stopped by a quaint little coffee shop called the Wicked Brew. So, stopping for coffee wasn't such a big deal after all. She couldn't help but smile. He didn't say a word when he jumped out of the truck and went inside. But, he wasn't gone long.

"Here you go," he said as he opened the door, sliding back into his seat, and handed her a latte. "Iced, skinny latte, two pumps vanilla, stirred, light on the ice. Best coffee in Moon Bay."

He remembered.

"Wow. Thank you. I'm shocked you remembered."

He tapped his temple and she noted his manicured fingers. Long fingers. "I never forget anything."

His smile melted her heart. She could get used to this. And to him.

"We're only about a mile away from the hotel, so we'll be there in no time."

She nodded and took a sip of her coffee. It was delicious, even better than her favorite shop in California.

"Mmmm. This is really good."

"A little old lady owns the shop. She also makes a mean danish. We'll have to get some for breakfast."

Breakfast. With him. That sounded more delicious than the idea of a sickeningly sweet bun. And she loved pastries. The sweeter the better. But yet, she had to keep reminding herself that he was only here to protect her. Nothing more. But her mind kept wandering.

As they slowly made their way to the hotel and she could see it in the distance, her anxiety about coming here started to ease. Her assistant knew her well. The hotel was right on the beach. Her own private slice of heaven.

Gregor pulled into the circular driveway of a glitzy hotel with a large backlit sign illuminating the name, The Breeze, in sweeping letters. He put the Tahoe in park and jumped out, snagging a luggage cart and loading up her belongings. He waved off the doorman that rushed over to help, then tossed his keys to the waiting valet and accepted the ticket he offered.

Krista started to get out, but he shook his head no, and then said something to the valet before coming to open her door. "Put on your glasses and hat. We don't want anyone knowing you're here. At least not yet."

She nodded, and then took his outstretched hand, the touch heating her skin. What a gentleman. None of her other bodyguards had ever treated her like this. They'd never helped her out of the car. The most they did was push her behind their bulky frames to keep fans from grabbing at her, because some fans would take chunk of hair or a pound of flesh if they got close enough. But none of her security detail had ever treated her with the respect Gregor was showing. It was nice.

He put his arm around her waist as they entered the hotel lobby, and then walked right past the counter and into a waiting elevator.

"Don't we have to check in?"

"We already are."

"We are?" She asked, surprised.

"I called from the Wicked Brew. And then I had the valet verify it for me while I got our stuff out of the truck. I didn't want the clerk or, anyone else, for that matter, to recognize you. The longer we can go without anyone finding out you're here, the better. Not only will you be happier. You'll be safer too."

"You really think of everything, don't you?" she said. And meant every word of it. She really was impressed.

"I try." He said. "Just doing my job."

She had to admit him saying he was just doing his job stung a little. It shouldn't, but it did.

She took another sip of her latte to cover her disappointment and waited for the elevator to stop at their floor. It didn't take long before the doors opened and revealed a short hallway leading to a spacious suite with two bedrooms, a living room with a huge comfortable-looking sectional sofa and at least a sixty-inch television. There was even a small kitchen. Not that she intended to cook anything. But it was a nice touch. There was a welcome basket on the countertop with fruit, cheese, and a few bottles of wine. The wine would come in handy. And of course, a coffee maker. That was one thing she couldn't live without. Huge windows overlooked the beach below and she could hear the crash of the waves. Hopefully, that sound would lull her to sleep at night.

With a quick peek around, Krista chose the larger of the two bedrooms, dropped her purse on the bed, took off her hat and sunglasses and placed them on the bureau. Sitting on the bed, she kicked off her shoes and rubbed the arches of her feet. After the aches eased away, she checked out the attached bathroom. One of the biggest soaker tubs available to man called to her. She'd put that to good use later tonight.

She turned around to find Gregor standing right behind her. How long had he been there? A flushed heat spread across her cheeks.

"Is everything to your liking?" He asked. "It's not the Four Seasons, but it's the nicest place in Moon Bay."

"It's perfect. Thanks." She said, then just stared at him, a little taken aback.

Did he think she was that shallow? That if it wasn't the Four Seasons it wouldn't be good enough for her. Is that the aura she put out? That's not who she was. Or was it?

Along with working on this trip, she apparently had a lot of soul searching to do.

"Well, if you don't need me for anything, I'm going to unpack and get settled in. Did you want to meet for dinner?" Krista wanted to kick herself. He was her bodyguard, not her date. What was she thinking? Yet, she knew the answer. She was thinking about those rock-hard abs that were surely under that black silk dress shirt. She knew she wouldn't be disappointed if she ever got the chance to see him naked, not that she ever would. But boy, could she imagine it. And even in her imagination, he didn't disappoint.

This is exactly what Jessie had warned her about. She could not sleep with her security detail. She needed to remember that mantra. *I can't sleep with my bodyguard. I can't sleep with my bodyguard.* She'd been there, done that, received the medal. And each time it ended in heartbreak.

"There are some things I want to go over with you." He said, completely focused on business. 'I think we should just order room service tonight."

But she didn't want to be cooped up in her hotel room all night. She'd just spent hours on a plane and then a couple more stuck in the truck while they made their way to the hotel. Maybe if he settled in he would change his mind about dinner. "Do you want to go unpack and then come back?" Krista asked.

He snatched his duffel bag off the luggage rack and headed into the second bedroom.

Krista rushed towards him. "Um," she didn't know what to say, other than, 'what the Hell are you doing?"

"I'm unpacking."

She laughed. "Yeah, I see that. Don't you have your own room?"

"Yes, I'm taking the smaller one."

"No, I mean, your own room. In your own suite?"

"I can't protect you if I'm in another part of the hotel. We're sharing this suite."

"You've got to be kidding me. You can't stay here."

He continued into his bedroom, ignoring her protests. "Don't worry, my intentions are strictly professional," he called over his shoulder before closing the door.

IT TOOK ALL of Gregor's strength to keep his composure. He didn't think sharing a suite with Krista Wallingford would be a big deal, but, then he saw her.

She was gorgeous and the fit of his trousers became tighter every time he looked at her. That never happened to him. Ever. So, what was it about her that he found so intriguing? He had no idea. But the even bigger question was, how was he going to keep their relationship platonic? Because, damn him if he was wrong, but she seemed interested in him, too. This assignment was going to be harder than he ever expected. He swore after what happened to Katherine, he'd never get involved with a client again. He planned to keep that vow.

He'd have to concentrate on the task at hand and not on the pretty redhead just outside the door, huffing and puffing because they were sharing a suite.

To get her out of his mind, if only for a moment, he decided to unpack. He put his carefully folded clothes, along with his socks and underwear, in the dresser drawers, then took his two suits out of the garment bag and hung them up in the closet. Shoes went on the closet floor, placed in a neat row. He could breathe now. Everything was in its place.

He put his toiletries and shaving bag in the bathroom and looked at himself in the mirror. His ice-blue eyes were swirling with color as they always did. If Krista had noticed, she hadn't said anything.

If she was upset about sharing a suite with him, he couldn't imagine her reaction if she found out he wasn't human. Well, not true. He was half human thanks to his mother, but the other half, was all gargoyle.

Being a bodyguard was the perfect line of work for someone like him. His species were born to protect.

And when it came to his job, he was the best. No one compared. He'd been working as a bodyguard in California for the past ten years and had grown quite the reputation with the Hollywood elite as the go-to guy for all matters involving security.

It was why he'd been hired to protect Krista. She'd received some disturbing items in the mail. Not that she would admit to it. She'd convinced herself that things like this came with the job, frightening or not, but that it was just a part of being an actress. Something she had to endure.

Not on his watch.

He could promise her that.

Images of Katherine's lifeless body seeped into his mind and he winced.

That would not happen again. He'd die before he'd let harm come to another one of his clients.

AN HOUR LATER, Gregor and Krista sat at the small table eating the food they'd ordered from room service. Gregor opened a bottle of red wine the hotel management had left for them, and Krista wondered if he could feel her eyes on him as he worked the corkscrew.

Watching as his muscles flexed and bunched.

He poured her a glass, handed it to her, then set the bottle down on the table between them.

"None for you?"

"I'm on the clock." He answered. I'm fine with water."

"We're not going anywhere tonight. Why don't you kick back and relax?"

"I'm good." He uncapped the bottle of Pellegrino and took a swallow. "Now, tell me what's been happening with this stalker of yours."

Krista shrugged. "There's not much to tell, really. If I'm being honest, I don't even think I have a stalker."

Gregor's stare bored into her, letting her know he wasn't buying her bullshit. "I was hired for a reason."

She worked her lower lip. "Weird things just started happening all of a sudden. I don't think any particular thing was a catalyst for it."

"What sort of things?"

She blew out a breath. She didn't want to talk about this. She really didn't. "It's no big deal."

"It is a big deal." Gregor said, and sat back in his chair staring at her. "And I need you to be completely honest with me. No more bullshit."

Krista took another swallow of wine and sighed. "Fine. I've received flowers. Cards. Stuff like that. Nothing threatening."

"I'll be the judge of that." He said. "Any messages?"

"Sometimes. At first, they were innocent enough, just telling me he liked my work, and that he couldn't wait to see what I would do next." She sipped her wine and paused. "Then they got a bit more...creepy, I guess you'd call it."

"Creepy how?"

"It was as if he was watching me. He'd talk about seeing me on set. Asking me out. Saying he wanted me to pay more attention to him."

"You never saw him?"

Krista shook her head. "Never. At least, not that I know of."

"And you don't have any idea who it is?"

"Not a clue."

She watched as he took a long pull from the bottle of water. Weirdly fascinated as his Adam's apple bobbed up and down with each swallow. She wanted to reach out and touch his neck. Kiss him. Feel those powerful arms holding her close.

He possessed this raw power that held itself in check just under the surface. Yet, she had the feeling that if someone pissed him off, they'd be on their ass in seconds flat.

A knock at the door pulled Krista out of her thoughts, and she jumped up to answer it, but Gregor held her back with a strong arm. "I'll get it." He said, then crept toward the door and peered through the peephole.

"Is it the boogey man?" she asked half-heartedly.

He pierced her with an icy gaze.

"This is nothing to joke about."

He didn't move for a few minutes while he looked through the peephole, but then he finally relented and opened the door.

Krista peered around him but didn't see anything or anyone even when Gregor bent over and picked something up. She still didn't see anything when he stepped into the hall and looked in both directions. Damn. He really was serious. She honestly didn't think all the precautions were necessary. But he was her bodyguard. And according to Jessica, the best one out there.

Finally, he closed the door behind him, and set a box on the table.

"Are those chocolates?" She reached for the box, but he halted her with a stern look.

"These could be from *him*."

"Or," she drew out the word, "more than likely, the production company sent them over as a welcome gift."

"If that were the case, why wouldn't they wait for someone to answer the door?" Gregor asked.

"Who knows. I'm not the only actor in this movie. Maybe they're making their rounds. Or, they sent a courier."

"I don't like it." He said. "Not one bit. Don't touch it. If it's from him, we'll need to have it analyzed."

"Seriously? You are such a buzz kill." She slumped onto the leather couch, sinking into the thick cushions. "Do what you need to do. I don't really need candy anyway. I'll stick to wine." Grabbing the remote, she clicked on the television and channel surfed. He was going to do whatever he thought needed to be done. So, she was going to let him.

Even if she did think he was being way over the top about the whole thing.

She clicked through multiple channels before settling on a cupcake cooking competition. These kids baking skills put Krista's to shame. Thank God for catering. She continued to watch as their cupcakes transformed into masterpieces that even a well-skilled baker would have a hard time replicating.

"Here." Gregor held out the box of chocolates. "You can eat them to your heart's content."

Krista pierced him with a questioning glare but said nothing.

"You were right."

"Excuse me?" She lifted her brow and smirked.

"These are from the production company." He waited for her to accept the candy before heading to his room. "Enjoy."

FEELING like an ass for the way he acted, Gregor was trying to keep his distance from Krista. Maybe giving her some space would help to cool things down. Especially their tempers. He'd pissed her off and that was never his intent. He was here to keep her safe. Plain and simple. This was a job. Nothing else. He needed to keep his head in the game and his eye on the end zone.

He sighed. Gods above, she was beautiful. He'd been security detail for plenty of beautiful actresses. But none of them affected him the way Krista did. The thought of her had his cock stirring. It'd been way too long since he'd slept with a woman.

He ran his hands through his short hair. Damn. He needed a cold shower. Frustrated didn't even begin to explain how he was feeling right now. And if right now was any indication, he would need a lot more cold showers in the future. He had no idea how long it would take Krista to finish filming her movie. Or how long it would take him to find and put Thaddeus away. Just the thought of being this close to her for any length of time had him hard as a rock. His clothes were restricting, so he stripped on his way to the bathroom. The shower was helping to simmer the blood pumping through his veins, but being back in Moon Bay had flooded him with memories. Reminding him of things that were long overdue, like reconnecting with his brother, Gunther.

It'd been a while since he talked to him and years since he'd seen him. Any communication they had always ended in a fight. His brother was far too much like his father. Opinionated and egotistical.

He stood there, unmoving, letting the water run over him. Cooling his heated skin.

Trying to wash Krista out of his mind was an impossible task. Until they caught this crazy bastard, and he was back in his own home, he'd have to be near her. With her. Twenty-four hours a day. How the hell was he going to keep a clear head?

Maybe he should bow out. Find someone else to do the job. But there was no denying he was the best. It wouldn't be fair to Krista if he let someone less skilled protect her. He would never forgive himself if something happened to her.

Besides, he never backed down from a challenge. Surrender wasn't in his nature.

With his mind made up, he quickly finished his shower, dressed in sweats and a tee, then walked out to the kitchenette to make some coffee. He craved something stronger, but he was working. There'd be time for that shit later.

Krista wasn't watching television on the couch anymore. He listened for sounds coming from her room but heard nothing. Maybe she was taking a nap.

It was his turn to give the T.V. a go, so he grabbed the remote off the side table and sat down with his coffee and spent the next forty-five minutes channel surfing, waiting for Krista to reappear.

Periodically he glanced at her bedroom door. Tempted to knock. To make sure she was okay and not too upset.

An hour later there was still no sign of her.

CHAPTER FIVE

Thaddeus's file was pretty slim on details. Gregor had a description and a picture, but he didn't need more than that. The details of skin walker were forever emblazoned in his memory.

Being a skin walker, the picture was useless. If Thaddeus was trying to get to Krista, he had to know The Guardians were after him, so he'd be stupid to stay in his own skin.

A note scribbled on the file said that Thaddeus had kept his nose clean after retirement and was liked by the other residents. He wasn't troublemaker in Hillsview, the city demons retired to when they were ready, so for all intents and purposes, he seemed like the perfect retiree. But his infatuation with Krista was unhealthy. Creepy even. He wanted her to believe that the supernatural existed. Who knows why? But people had done crazier things for less. He thought about it for a minute, then tossed the folder onto the coffee table and took in a long drawn out breath. Thaddeus's obsession of Krista was very reminiscent of his feelings for Katherine. Once again, he regretted not getting to the skin walker before he'd been returned to Hillsview after Katherine's death.

He couldn't handle this alone. As much as he hated it, he was going to need some help. So, even though it pricked at his pride, he knew it was time to call in the big guns.

Gregor hadn't talked to his brother in years, but he was on the Moon Bay police force. Who better to help him with his case? He hadn't bothered to tell his family that he'd be in town, but chances were they already knew, especially since he was here by command of The Superior Council. Either way, Gunther would be his best way to find out what was happening around town.

Gregor flipped through the contacts on his cell phone and hit the number for his brother. Gunther answered on the third ring.

"Magnuson."

"Gunth, it's me."

"Well, now, little bro. To what do I owe this pleasure? What's the occasion?"

His brother was an ass. And a sarcastic one at that. He was just jealous because Gregor had been made a Dark Moor Guardian instead of him. It was something he'd been bitter about ever since, completely ignoring the fact that their sister, Rona, had also made the cut. But he would never get over it.

"I'm good. Thanks for asking. How are you?"

"I'm hanging in there." Gregor heard papers rustling. "What do you want? I've got work to do. You know these humans can be a real pain in the ass."

Gregor chuckled. It was obvious his brother wasn't in the mood to talk. Fine. He'd keep it short and sweet.

"Actually, this is work related and has to do with Moon Bay. I'm hoping you can provide me with some insight."

"You here?"

He was pretty sure his brother already knew that he was in Moon Bay, but he'd have to answer to him anyway.

"I am. Arrived earlier today." The silence between them lasted longer than he would have liked, as if Gunther was thinking about what he should say next. A question Gregor knew was coming before he even asked it.

"Does Dad know?"

"I haven't reached out to him." Gregor cringed. "I'm working." Did he sound as petty to Gunther, as he did to his own ears? Probably. But Gunther knew how deep the divide was between him and their dad, though he never stopped busting Gregor's balls about it. It wasn't all his dad's fault. Gregor owned his share of the blame, and he understood that Gunther wanted them to work it out, but sometimes there was just too much water under the bridge. In their case, an ocean. And he _was_ working even if he knew deep down it really wasn't a legitimate excuse. He should have reached out to them when he found out he would be in Moon Bay.

But he'd never admit it.

"Ah, that's right. Gregor Magnuson, bodyguard to the stars." Gregor flinched at the harshness in his brother's voice.

"You know, Gunth, if you think about it, our jobs really aren't all that different."

"Do you have a degree?" His brother paused, waiting. "Yeah, I didn't think so."

Gregor sighed and pinched the bridge of his nose. Why did their conversations always turn into a pissing match? "Congratulations. You win." He waited to see if his brother would throw another snide remark his way and continued when he didn't. "I'm in town guarding Krista Wallingford while she films her latest movie."

"Tough gig. That must be dreadful. So, you need help dealing with her? She too much for you?"

"Real funny." Gregor said, and rolled his eyes, so sick of

this attitude his brother was giving him. "The assignment came from The Council. I wasn't hired by her."

"Of course it did. So, who is it this time?"

"Thaddeus."

"The skin walker?" His brother's voice trailed off. "He's here?"

"Maybe."

"Damn." He could almost see Gunther shaking his head, as if he were sitting right in front of him and not just on the other end of the phone line.

"He was in L.A." Gregor said. "But he's been stalking her. So, I'm sure he'll follow her here, if he hasn't already. Have you seen him?"

"Can't say that I have. But I haven't been looking either. My days are filled with over-indulging vacationers."

"Would you mind keeping an eye out?" Gregor asked. "And let me know if you see or hear anything? He's been sending her some weird shit. And she has no idea who he is." Gregor paused and took a deep breath. "So far, she doesn't seem to believe in our existence."

"She doesn't know you're a gargoyle?"

"She doesn't know about any of it."

"That's fucked up, man. Anyway, I gotta get back to work, but I'll keep an eye out and let you know if I spot him." His brother paused. "You gonna reach out to Dad?"

Gregor threw his head back and blew out a breath. "I will." He said, then ended the call and set the folder aside. It didn't really do him much good anyway. This was going to take a hell of a lot of footwork.

An hour and another pot of coffee later and Krista still hadn't come out of her room.

Gregor was no psychic, but he was beginning to think he was alone in the suite. There was still no noise coming from

Krista's room and she didn't strike him as the type of person to stay quiet for such a long time.

He knocked on her door, loudly.

No answer.

He listened.

Nothing.

"If you don't open this door in five seconds, I'm coming in," he called out, giving her fair warning.

Still nothing.

"Five, four, three, two, one." No movement. "Time's up." He turned the knob and opened the door to an empty room. "Shit!" He checked the bathroom. She wasn't in there either.

"Son of a bitch." He rushed into his bedroom, grabbed his keys, then reached into his pocket for his phone and dialed Krista's number. It went straight to voicemail.

She turned off her phone?

Gregor was irate. His vision clouded, his body's urge to shift to his gargoyle form strong.

He'd never let a charge give him the slip before. Ever. This wasn't good. He was going to need help. And as much as it pained him to do it, he dialed his brother's number. "Wow, I don't hear from you in forever, and then here you are, twice in one day." His brother answered, sarcastic as usual.

"She's missing."

"Who?"

"The Queen Mother. Who do you think? Krista."

"How'd you manage that one, bro?" He laughed. "What was that? I couldn't make out the mumbling."

Gregor sighed. "I said, she gave me the slip."

"Now, that is priceless."

"Can you help?"

"Hold on." He heard muffled voices as his brother covered the phone receiver with his hand as he spoke to someone in the room. "Looks like we might have some suspicious activity over at Neon Waves."

"What type of activity? And what is Neon Waves?"

"It's a club and apparently, a woman was found passed out in the bathroom."

"How is that not normal? It's a club."

"Because she's telling everyone that will listen that a guy attacked her as she came out of a stall and stole her face."

That was interesting. "Think it's Thaddeus?"

"You know any other skin walkers roaming around?"

"Fuck."

"Then I'd say it's probably the work of your guy. I'm heading over there now if you want to meet me. I'll text you the address."

KRISTA SLIPPED OUT of the hotel and took a deep breath, inhaling the salty air then glanced back at the lobby, half-expecting Gregor to be stalking up behind her.

Giving him the slip proved to be a cakewalk. She was beginning to question his security skills. Getting away unnoticed was way too easy, especially for someone who was supposed to be the best in the business. Because tonight, he was severely lacking.

Krista shrugged. What could it hurt to have a little time for herself? Everyone needed time alone now and again. She enjoyed her freedom just like the next person and with filming starting soon she wouldn't have much time to spare. And it wasn't like she was going out to do something dangerous. She'll probably just have a drink or two. Hell, she might even dance. Moon Bay had to have a decent club or two nearby. Tonight, she just wanted to forget about everything.

She seriously doubled that her weirdo stalker had

followed her here, but just to be safe, she wore a blonde wig and fixed her makeup to give her a whole new look. She even changed the color of her eyes with the help of a pair of blue contacts.

Two women, dressed in their best club-wear exited the lobby. It was obvious that they were going out, or would at least know where she should go to have a good time. One of the women stopped near her, pausing to light a cigarette and inhaled deeply.

"Excuse me." Krista paused, and waited to see if they recognized her. They didn't, and she breathed a quick sigh of relief. "Could you tell me the best spot to grab some drinks? Maybe a place with some loud music and dancing?"

"Yeah, sure, we're on our way to Neon Waves. They've got awesome drinks and play a great range of music. They're always packed." She held out her hand, "I'm Jamie." She pointed to the woman beside her, "and this is Viv. We've called an Uber to take us there if you want to come along?"

"You don't mind?"

The women looked at one another and shrugged. "Not at all."

"Cool, I'm Kay, by the way," Krista answered, not wanting to give away her identity.

The car arrived a few minutes later and they all climbed in, and as it pulled away from the hotel, Krista noticed a man watching them as they left. Unease crawled over her, but what were the chances? It was more likely he saw three hot ladies on their way out and was checking out long legs, short skirts and stilettos.

"Where are you from?" Viv asked.

"Kansas." Not a lie. She'd lived there a long time ago for a couple of years.

"Vacation?"

Krista paused, she didn't feel like sharing her personal information. "Kind of."

Jamie smiled. "Ah, so mysterious. That's cool. I get that."

"Are you running from someone?" Viv questioned.

"What? No." Krista smirked. "Why do you ask?"

The brunette shrugged, "When you came out of the hotel, you kept looking back inside. Like you were waiting for someone to come after you."

She sighed. "That obvious, huh?"

Both women nodded.

Maybe she could play up this whole trying to get away scenario. "You know how it is. We had a fight and I needed to get out. He didn't agree and wanted me to stay with him." She lowered her voice. "I had to wait until he fell asleep so I could sneak out."

"Living on the edge. How do you manage?" Jamie asked sarcastically.

Okay, so maybe they didn't buy her story. Whatever. The car pulled into the club's parking lot and they all climbed out. They could believe what they wanted. For now, she was out of Gregor's sight.

"Thanks for the ride." She dug around in her purse, found a twenty-dollar bill and handed it to Jamie, the least she could do since they'd let her bum a ride.

Once inside, Krista headed straight for the bar. She really wanted a margarita and the drink of the night happened to be a tropical version. Perfect. The dark-haired bartender wasn't too bad either. *Hello, Moon Bay.*

The pounding music vibrated through her body. The constant thrum had her bouncing her way to a table in the far corner. She usually liked being the center of attention, but for once, she just wanted to sit and enjoy her drink, and watch the crowd. Maybe dance to a song or two.

"You can't just sit there." Jamie appeared in front of her.

"Come dance with us!" She grabbed Krista's hand and pulled her around the table and onto the crowded dance floor. Space was at a minimum but when one of her favorite songs started playing, she couldn't help but dance.

She let everything go and started swaying to the music, moving her hips from side to side in rhythm with the beat. She lifted her arms and then went low, slowly raising up, dragging her hands along her legs as she went. She spun and then whipped her hair around.

This was fun. Viv and Jamie danced alongside her until they were all out of breath and made their way back to Krista's table, collapsing in their chairs.

"Thanks, you guys. You have no idea how much I needed a night away."

Jamie jumped up. "Drinks are on me. What do you want?" The bouncy blonde left with their drink orders and she and Viv watched the dancers while they waited.

"I'm having a great time." Krista giggled. "This is a great spot."

A few minutes later, they were all sipping their margaritas, and scanning the crowd for potential hook-ups. Well, for Jamie and Viv.

Krista couldn't get her mind off Gregor. She could imagine his big body sidling up to hers. His large hands on her hips as she swung them seductively and dangerously close to his groin.

She cleared her throat. Okay, enough fantasizing about Gregor. If he caught her here, the last thing on his mind would be sleeping with her, she was damn sure of that.

SHE WAS MAKING this way too easy.

Thaddeus knew she wouldn't stay cooped up in her hotel

room. He was glad he'd parked facing the lobby doors of The Breeze because he was able to get a good look at the two women she hopped into a car with.

He kept his distance from the trio as he'd followed them to the club. It was a monstrosity of neon lights and loud, thumping music that he could hear through the open car window.

He waited for them to enter the building and then found a place to park. He spotted a hip, young stud in the parking lot getting ready to leave. After making eye contact, he took on the guy's appearance, and then sauntered up to the entrance, hoping they didn't ask for identification, or he'd have to turn around and leave. Potentially missing out on making contact with Krista. He let out the breath he'd been holding when they didn't bother to ID him and only asked for the cover charge. Twenty-five American dollars. Damn. Must be one hell of a party.

Thaddeus walked into a nightmare. Lights of all colors strobed constantly, flashing on the floor, walls and ceiling, which were painted black to reflect the colors better. High tables lined the walls. There was no sitting room. The floor throbbed with the loud techno music humans these days seemed to enjoy so much. Couples writhed together on the dance floor, but he paid them little attention.

He spotted the three women, drinks in hand and watched from the shadows, just waiting for the right moment to make his move. And he didn't have to wait long. Thaddeus followed the brunette toward the back of the club as she made her way to the ladies' room, keeping a short distance between them.

After she entered the restroom, he waited to make sure no one followed her in. When the coast was clear, he quietly slipped in behind her. A quick sweep of the stalls and he was sure it was just the two of them.

He stood off to the side, by a long bank of sinks, and like he had hoped, she didn't notice him when she first emerged from the stall, it wasn't until she reached the sink to wash her hands that awareness sparked.

He just needed her to look directly into his eyes. She granted him his wish as her eyes widened with surprise, and then fear as he shifted his outer appearance to mimic hers. Fast as lightning, he was behind her, his arm tightening around her throat, constricting her air until she lost consciousness.

He dragged her limp body into the furthest stall and propped her up on the toilet. He grabbed the purse she had wrapped around her wrist and left the stall, clicking the lock in place when he closed the door. Digging around in her purse, he found a stick of red lip stain and reapplied the color to his own lips. Damn, he liked this body. Not enough to keep it, but it'd serve his purpose well.

CHAPTER SIX

The drinks flowed easily, and Krista was enjoying her time with her new friends. Jamie had wandered onto the dance floor with a total surfer dude and had pretty much stayed there ever since.

Viv was cool, though. They were connecting and having a great time. Krista thought about Gregor and felt the slightest tinge of guilt. Did he know she was gone yet? He was going to be really pissed once he figured it out.

"Hey, you wanna get out of here?" Viv broke into her thoughts. "I know another cool spot."

Krista searched for Jamie in the mob of dancers.

"Don't worry about Jamie. She'll be fine. We do this all the time."

Krista bit her lower lip. She was torn. She knew if the roles were reversed, she wouldn't want to be left behind.

"I'm gonna go talk to her and make sure she's all set. Be right back." Viv finished the last sip of her drink and went to talk to Jamie, who looked over at Krista and waved excitedly.

She took that as a sign that Jamie was okay with them

leaving so when Viv returned, Krista grabbed her purse and finished off her own drink. "Ready if you are."

"Am I ever. Let's go."

Krista gave a final wave and followed Viv to the front of the club, squeezing between other patrons as they went.

Gregor's hulking figure met her at the door, and she stopped dead in her tracks. His mouth was set in a grim line. Pissed off didn't even begin to explain the look on his face.

Viv stiffened beside her.

"It's okay, Viv, he's not here for you." She sighed, resigned to the fact that her fun night was over.

A police officer almost the size of Gregor walked through the door right on his heels. Something was definitely going on. They were not just searching for her, because the other man looked awfully official as he sized her up and continued to look around the club, but, wasn't hard putting two and two together to realize they were related.

Seriously? Gregor *would* have relatives working in Moon Bay's PD.

She turned to say something to Viv and realized the woman was nowhere to be found. "Viv?" She called out, but her friend had disappeared.

"Who's Viv? Wait, you can tell me later." Gregor said, then grabbed her arm and began to pull her toward the door. "Right now, I need to get you out of here."

"Wait!" She yanked her arm back, planting her feet. "Stop manhandling me."

"Do you realize how much danger you're in?"

"None until you walked in. You've ruined a perfectly fun girls' night."

"He's here."

"Who?" Krista asked and then understanding dawned on her and she felt all the blood drain from her face. "How?"

"I don't know. Did you see anyone hanging around you? Clinging more than usual?"

"Gregor, it's a club. It's all about clinging."

"You could've been hurt."

"Why? If you lose me, you won't get paid?"

"It has nothing to do with money. What the hell were you thinking taking off without saying a word?"

She scoffed. "So you could tell me to stay put. No thank you."

"You have no idea how much danger you're in."

"And you," she shoved a finger into his rock-hard chest, "are a major buzz-kill."

Gregor looked to the cop that was silently watching their exchange.

Krista shifted her attention to him. "Can you tell this man," she spit the word out, "to leave me alone?"

He cleared his throat and stepped up to her, his outstretched hand reaching for hers. "Officer Magnuson, ma'am. But you can call me Gunther."

She drew in a breath, praying for patience. "First, don't ever call me ma'am. I'm not my mother. Second, can you do your job and arrest this man for harassing me?"

"I see you've met my little brother."

There was nothing little about Gregor Magnuson.

"Great. So, in other words, I can expect no help from you." She spun, ready to make her way into the night.

"Actually," Gunther stepped forward. "There's a situation going on in the back that I need to attend to. A call came in while I was talking to Gregor and might be related to some of the issues you've been dealing with."

"Ah, so that's what we're calling them now. Issues." She put her hands up and made air quotes when she spoke.

Gunther had the wherewithal to look away.

"Krista," Gregor approached, his hands stuck like glue to

his sides. "A woman was attacked in the ladies room. We think it might be related."

"Why? I wasn't attacked. Don't you think it would be me getting attacked if it was related to me?" Gregor and Gunther exchanged a mysterious look that she couldn't decipher. "Don't play games with me."

Gunther excused himself to deal with whatever it was he thought may or may not be related to her stalker, leaving her alone with Gregor, who was clearly hiding something.

She planted her hands on her hips and looked up at the incorrigible man. "Something else is going on. What is it?" She paused, but the big oaf said nothing. Just looked at her with an unreadable expression on his beautiful face. "Why won't you tell me?" She asked, exasperation making her voice pitchy.

THE WHOLE CREED of The Guardians revolved around keeping the human world blissfully ignorant to all the super-natural wonders the world held. He was tempted to tell Krista. To make her understand. But it went against every-thing he'd sworn to.

Gunther sent him a quick shake of his head, warning him to stay quiet. Gregor agreed. Now was not the time.

"My job is to keep you safe. You make that very difficult when you're sneaking out and putting yourself into dangerous situations." His voice was stern. He felt like he was disciplining a child.

Her chocolate brown eyes pinned him with a look that told him he knew exactly why she did what she did. Gods above, this woman was going to be the death of him. "It was drinks and some dancing, Gregor. Nothing happened."

"Yet."

"What do you mean, yet? I'm here, aren't I? All in one piece." She spun around, arms out, as if to prove to him that she was fine.

"Where were you going?" He asked, trying to keep the fierceness he felt inside from tingeing his voice.

"What?" She spat, the word filled with irritation.

"When I got here. You were on your way out. Where were you going and with who?"

She had the look of someone caught doing something bad, then glanced around. Was she searching for someone?

Krista shrugged, ivory skin peeking from the shirt that had slipped off her shoulder. Skin his eyes were drawn to, imagining the softness. *Get a grip, man.* Fuck. He needed to remember what he was doing. He was working. And work didn't include sleeping with his charge. But damn, he'd guarantee that would be so fucking hot.

"...I was going to have a look around the city. There has to be more than one club." He'd missed the first part of her answer since he was too busy thinking of all the things he'd like to do to her.

What was it about Krista? It'd been years since he was even slightly interested in one of his clients. Not since, well, he didn't want to think about that.

"So, I guess you're going to drag me back to the hotel now, right? Hello? Welcome to the 21st century."

"Gregor," Gunther dipped his head to the side in a cue to join his brother, then he stopped an officer that was passing by. "Can you keep an eye on her for a while? Make sure she doesn't leave."

At the cop's nod, he left to go find Gunther, but not before Krista got in one last jab.

"You're such a Neanderthal." She closed her tiny fists and pounded her ample chest, grunting. "Woman. Mine."

He would have laughed if he hadn't been so shocked to

find out she thought he was acting like a caveman. Even if she did look ridiculously cute. And kiss-worthy.

IN A BACK ROOM at Neon Waves, Gregor listened as his brother interviewed the young woman who'd been attacked in the ladies' room, as bass from the techno music pulsed through the walls.

The woman was petrified. She'd also been drinking heavily and that would work out well for them. They could credit what she thought she saw to the alcohol. He had to give his brother props for how he handled her. He stayed calm, coaxing all the details from her and then managing to make her believe it was her intoxicated brain playing tricks on her.

Gunther stood and motioned for him to follow. "Did you catch it? The skin walker's scent is all over her. "

Gregor nodded. "Let's go." They followed the shifter's scent through the club and outside. It mixed with the night air but stood out like a shining beacon. It led them to the outer section of the parking lot, where it became fainter.

"The bastard must've left when he saw us come in. I lifted that scent faintly on Krista. The fucker has definitely made contact." Gregor couldn't believe the turn of events. Not only had Krista given him the slip, but the skin walker had actually been close enough to leave his mark on her. More than likely he'd talked to her and she didn't have a fucking clue who she was dealing with. He let out a guttural growl and punched the nearest tree, causing the trunk to shake and leaves to fall.

"We'll get him. Don't go losing your shit about it now. Keep your head straight, man."

"It's not that. I know I'll get him. It's just that I could smell him on Krista. It was faint, but it was there. He knows she's here."

Gunther swept his gaze from side to side. "Thaddeus is out there somewhere. He's probably watching us now, if I'd wager a guess."

"Agreed." Gregor scanned the lot.

"He's gotta know The Guardians are after him?"

"I'm sure. He'd be stupid not to." Gregor said, sighing. "Krista's going to draw him out, so I've just got to be vigilant. She can't go out alone." He swept his hand over his hair. "If she thought I was bad before, she's really going to be irritated now."

"I've got a few officers that I know can keep a secret. But her disguise worked because none of them know who she really is. If you want them, they're yours."

"Now look who wants to be Mr. Helpful."

"Yeah, well, don't let it go to your head. You'll still leave when all is said and done and we'll go back to not talking to each other."

Gregor gave his brother a genuine smile. For the first time in a long time, he didn't feel like he wanted to throat punch him. It was progress.

CHAPTER SEVEN

Back in the hotel room, Krista rummaged through her bags looking for some ibuprofen. A hell of a headache threatened and she wanted to try to stop it before it turned into a full-blown migraine. On the other side of the door, Gregor moved around in the kitchen, the cabinet doors opening and closing, the sound muffled through the walls.

The man was a brute. He seriously thought they were living in the Dark Ages the way he was going on about how she had to listen to what he said. That she couldn't go anywhere on her own.

Damn it. This was the twenty-first century. She was a modern woman for God's sake.

She didn't think men like him still existed. Oh, she knew, hot men like him existed, although he was in a league of his own. She'd never seen anyone that could even come close. And she'd seen a lot of guys. Had kissed a lot of men. Part of the job description and all. But damn, while he was lecturing her on their way back to the hotel, she couldn't concentrate on anything but his beautiful mouth forming words.

What words, she had no idea. She wasn't listening. But, she could imagine all the places she'd like his mouth to be. And forming words were the last thing she wanted him doing with those lips.

She sighed and flopped on the bed, bottle in hand. They hadn't even been together for a full twenty-four hours. How in the Hell did she already have it so bad?

Instant attraction is real, kids. She laughed, but the noise jarred her head. She needed water. She looked in her bathroom for a glass, but there wasn't one.

"Crap." She'd have to go out and grab one from the kitchen.

She opened the door and ran face first into a hard chest, stumbling back as Gregor tried to catch her from falling. She slapped his arms away and landed hard on her ass.

"What the hell are you doing?"

"Are you alright?" A look of concern marred his handsome face as he looked from her to the floor where a puddle of water was spreading. "I was bringing you these." He held out his hand and offered her two red pills. Ibuprofen, of course. He pushed past her and grabbed a towel from her bathroom and came back to wipe the water that had spilled. Luckily, the glass didn't break.

"I'm fine." She bit her lower lip, catching the corner with her tooth. "Thank you." Maybe he wasn't such a Neanderthal after all. "Sorry about the mess. I didn't expect you there."

"Well, to be fair, I didn't expect you to come charging out of your room like a woman on a mission, either. Did you need something?"

"We were thinking alike. I was on my way to get a glass so I could get some water and take a pill or two. My head's starting to pound."

He nodded, a knowing look crossing his face. "I figured. Here." He held out his hand for her to grasp, so he could pull her up. His hand was huge when she placed hers in his. It was easily three times the size of hers. Damn. You know what they said. Big hands...she glanced at his tennies, big feet...big --, she had to stop this line of thinking. It was detrimental to her sanity.

"I, uh," he pointed to the hall and started to back through the door out into the hallway. "I'm just going to go back and watch television or something."

"Okay. I'm going to grab some water and head to bed. Try to sleep this off."

He nodded and turned, walking away and leaving her feeling all alone. Weird, he just went into the other room. But, yet, the air in her room suddenly felt cold and empty.

GREGOR MINDLESSLY FLIPPED through the channels, not really seeing what was on, instead he was thinking about Krista running into his chest over and over again. She was so close. He almost reached out and kissed her. Not cool.

He blew out an exasperated breath.

But she was so soft. And close. And beautiful. Fuck. His cock twitched, letting Gregor know where it stood with the situation.

It's been one fucking day, dude.

Christ, you'd think he was a teenaged boy standing naked in the wind. This job was going to be the death of him. He needed to keep her at arm's length. Something he felt was going to be far easier said than done.

He heard her bare feet pad into the kitchen. Listened as she opened the cabinet and got a glass and filled it with water. He listened to her sip, swallowing the pills.

Damn it.

This was ridiculous. He jabbed the power button on the

TV to turn it off and went into his room, heading for the shower. He needed another cold one. Ice cold.

He turned the setting to cold and flipped the water on, and stripped down, as his cock bobbed to attention. Stepping into the frigid water didn't even have an impact. He was still hard as a rock. Goose bumps popped up on his skin as he let the water run over him, but his cock was still begging for relief, so he grasped his shaft, gave a few strokes up and down, but it did nothing. The only thing that would suffice was Krista. Her riding him while he held her hips was what he really wanted.

Frustrated, he turned the water off. It was going to be a long fucking night.

KRISTA TOSSED and turned throughout the night, jumping between dreams of Gregor wrapping his strong arms around her and pulling her close and some grotesque creature enveloping her in its long, scaly arms, whispering words that she couldn't quite make out.

The pain in her head had lessened to a dull thrum. Still there, but manageable. She kicked off the sheet, the cool air of the a/c blowing over her, raising goosebumps on her skin. Sleep was an uncertainty. Even as tired as she was, with the odd visions that kept invading her dreams, she would rather stay awake.

A flash of light outside drew her attention, followed by a crack of thunder that made her yelp. The loudness taking her by surprise. A few minutes later, a steady staccato of rain beat on the window. She listened and waited for the brilliant bolts of light, then counted the seconds until the thunder came.

The storm was close. She got up, opened the curtain and

pulled the chair close so she could sit in the dark and watch the storm play over the water.

Haunting and beautiful at the same time.

As one flash illuminated the water, she swore she could see someone on the white sands below.

Crazy. As pretty as the storm was to watch, you wouldn't catch her out there. She remembered reading an article about how many people were struck by lightning in Florida every year.

With each subsequent flash the person came closer to the hotel. They'd probably realized how much danger they were in and were hauling ass inside.

Letting the sound of the rain pattering against the window lull her into a state of relaxation, Krista closed her eyes. This was even better than meditation. It wasn't long before sleep won the battle and she drifted off into a dream-filled sleep.

CHAPTER EIGHT

The strong aroma of fresh brewed coffee greeted Krista when she woke. She was still curled up in the chair by the window and her back screamed when she straightened out, trying to rid herself of the kinks.

Gregor was in the living room catching up on the news when she walked into the hall. He jumped to his feet when he saw her. His mama had taught him well. Always the perfect gentlemen.

"You can keep doing what you're doing. I'm just going to grab a cup of coffee. Did you hear the storm last night?"

"Yes, it was quite the noise maker."

"It was." She added cream to her mug and filled it with coffee. Gregor sat back down and turned his attention back to the television. She took a seat at the bar and grabbed her tablet. She needed to post a few photos from last night to her Instagram account. She should've done it last night, while she was drinking and dancing, but she didn't even think about it. At least she didn't wake up with a headache. Thanks to Gregor.

She scrolled through her social media, posted a few pics

and responded to a few fans. Nothing too personal, just an emoji here and there. If she answered everyone that ever reached out to her on social media, she'd never get anything done.

But, one of the messages caught her eye.

I saw you last night. Dancing with your new-found friends, looking like you were having a great time. You really should be more careful before going out. Make sure you have your muscle with you at all times. Don't worry. We'll meet again.

Chills ran down her spine as she read the message again. He saw her last night. How? She was disguised. No one knew she was here other than Gregor and the production company.

"Gregor." He looked over, alarm evident on his face when he saw her expression.

"What is it?" He asked and jumped up from his seat. "What's wrong?"

She pushed her tablet to him, tapping it with her index finger. "Look what I got." She paused and waited for him to read the passage. His brow furrowed.

"Who sent this?"

She shrugged. "It came in through a messaging app. The name is odd and has to be fake. No one's parents would ever saddle them with the name of Thaddie Paddie." She rolled her eyes. "Can you imagine going through school with that? No thank you."

"The profile picture is no help. It's just a generic image of a vampire." He rubbed the light stubble on his jaw. He hadn't shaved yet and Krista found the look very inviting. "Can I borrow this?"

He held up her tablet. "Sure."

"I'm going to call my brother. See if he can look into this and figure anything out. Maybe they have a cyber unit that could at least tell us the general vicinity of the poster."

GREGOR WASN'T ready to tell Krista that he knew exactly who Thaddie Paddie was. What kind of name was that anyway? He waited impatiently for his brother to answer the phone, so when it clicked to voicemail he swore under his breath.

Stalking to her room, he rapped his knuckles against the door. "Get dressed," he called through the door. "We're going to have to go down to the station."

"Give me some time." She yelled back. "I need to get ready!"

"You've got twenty minutes."

He started to walk away when she called out. "I need more than that." He opened his mouth to answer but was met with a loud blast of music which would've drowned out anything he had to say.

A growl escaped his lips and he went into the kitchen. He couldn't sit still while Thaddeus was out there, watching her every move.

Fucking skin walker. He was going to be difficult to find. But, if they could find the general area where he was staying, it'd be a little easier.

While he waited for Krista to do whatever it was that women do, he washed and dried their coffee cups, stacking them back in the cupboard before wiping down the counters. He tidied up the living room, which took all of thirty seconds. Then he folded up the newspaper and set it on the coffee table.

Still no sign of Krista. So, he went into his own room, and dressed in one of the suits he'd hung up in the closet. A dark blue Armani he matched with a crisp white shirt and smoke gray tie. Tightening the knot, he heard Krista emerge from her room.

He met her out in the hallway and felt a stab of pride at the appreciative look she blessed him with.

Her nod of approval something he didn't know he was longing for.

"Ready?"

Her chocolate eyes darkened to mocha at his question. Sexual tension hung heavy in the air. It was a good thing they were leaving. Gregor didn't trust himself to be alone with her at the moment.

AN HOUR LATER, Krista sat in a sparsely furnished conference room tucked deep into the underbelly of the Moon Bay Police Station. The room offered only a small semblance of privacy with its huge windows looking out into the dimly lit hallway and smelled like burnt coffee. She concentrated on studying the script that was delivered to her just before they left.

It was a character she'd portrayed before, being the third and final movie in the series. This time, her character moves to Florida to leave her old life behind after putting her tormentor away when she testified against him. Now he's managed to escape from an asylum he was being housed in after faking an illness and of course, he's trying to find her to seek his revenge.

She sipped her coffee, one they'd picked up on the way, thankfully, from Gregor's favorite coffee shop. Krista sighed. Lots of running. Lots of screaming. She loved these movies and had the genre to thank for making her one of the most sought-after actresses in Hollywood, but once, just once, she'd love to get a serious script. Something that didn't have characters coming back from the dead. At least this series was only a trilogy.

She'd love to snag an Oscar-worthy role. That would be amazing.

She kept reading, saying some of the lines aloud, practicing her cadence.

Gregor cleared his throat, and she looked up at him, his bulk filling the space of the doorframe. "Sorry, I don't want to disturb you."

She set the script on the table. "You're not. I'm just reading."

He glanced at the stack of papers. "We can go whenever you're ready." He entered the room and shut the door quietly behind him. "There's nothing else we can do here."

"So, what's the deal with you and your brother?"

He raised a golden eyebrow in question. "What do you mean?"

She shrugged. "I get the feeling that you two, um, what are the words?" She paused and tried to read Gregor's expression, but he was giving nothing away. "I don't know. That maybe you guys don't always get along."

"We have a long history. Lots of family drama that I won't bore you with by going into the details."

"Do you see each other often?"

He laughed at that. A deep, guttural sound that heated her insides.

"No. Before this trip, I hadn't seen Gunther in years."

"Because of the drama?"

"You could say that."

"Do you have other brothers and sisters?"

Gregor nodded, a look deepening the ice blue of his eyes. "I do. They're back home."

"Home?"

"Scotland," he said, a faraway look in his eyes. "I haven't been back in a really long time."

"Aha!" She exclaimed. "That's the faint accent I can hear in your voice. It was driving me crazy."

He gave her an odd look. "Really?"

"Mhmhm. Is the reason you haven't seen them work? My parents passed when I was young so I don't remember them. I grew up in the foster system, but I imagine it must be hard to be separated from your family."

"You could say that. It's been tough."

She had the feeling there was more to the story, but he didn't want to discuss it.

"In addition to Gunther, I've got another brother and two sisters."

"Wow, big family."

He sighed and she could sense he was getting uncomfortable with the conversation, so she changed the subject. "Are you ready to leave?"

"Yes. Gunth has someone looking into the message. Until then, me and you are like glue."

"Yeah. That's not going to happen. Tomorrow I need to report on set. There'll be plenty of security there."

"Including me."

The thought of Gregor shadowing her every movement was unsettling. She didn't doubt he'd provide her with more than adequate protection. It was the thought of him watching her scenes. And it shouldn't matter. It was her job. But there was a love scene in there.

Why did the thought of kissing someone else in front of Gregor upset her so much? They meant nothing to each other. And the last thing she needed was to fall for another bodyguard.

Been there. Done that. Won the trophy more times than she'd like to count.

"You can just drop me off at the set. I'll be fine."

"You <u>will</u> be fine." His beautiful lips formed a firm line. "Because <u>I'll</u> be there right beside you."

She sighed. There was no arguing with him. She snatched up the script before shoving it into her handbag and grabbing her coffee, then she stood in front of him waiting for him to open the door to let her out.

Now she remembered why she wanted to go out dancing so bad. Gregor was such an alpha male that Krista was pretty sure he didn't even realize how overbearing he was when doing his job.

CHAPTER NINE

The filming location the studio had chosen for this movie rated pretty high on the creepy factor. Most of Moon Bay was coastal with beautiful beaches. However, towards the outskirts of the city, there was a walking trail that brought you through marshes and thick patches of yucca plants on either side, ready to scratch and impale you if you weren't paying attention.

Pine needles and oak leaves littered the ground and the low-hanging moss from the mossy oaks added to the eeriness.

The further down the path you went, the further you were from civilization. Krista followed the director as he led the way, explaining about the different plants and what to stay away from.

"How about alligators? Are there any here?" She looked around nervously. The area looked like the perfect spot for them to hang around.

Gregor walked beside her and didn't seem the least bit worried that some dinosaur-type lizard would attack them.

"Not in this part," Rogan answered. "There's not enough water. Now, wild hogs, that's a different story."

Krista stopped dead in her tracks? "What?"

Rogan sighed. "It's Florida. There's a lot of wildlife here. But, don't worry. We've scoped out the area and we have the filming location fenced off. Nothing is getting in."

"And how about on the trek to get there? Did you ever think of that?"

Gregor had the audacity to look amused.

"I find nothing about this funny, Gregor."

"You'll be fine, Krista. But I'd keep walking. You don't want to give whatever's out there a chance to catch you."

Her eyes widened and he winked. He was teasing her. "Not funny." She punched his arm to let him know she wasn't happy with him, but regretted it as soon as her fist met his skin. It felt like she hit a concrete wall.

He looked down at her, a crooked grin brightening his face. "You okay?" He asked as she rubbed her knuckles.

She nodded and trudged forward. Man, she pitied the guy who tried to take Gregor on. He'd be in for a world of hurt.

They came to a fence and the group stopped as Rogan punched in the security code to let them all in. Inside the gates, the area was just as creepy as outside, but at least were protected from any wildlife that may be looking for dinner, or worse, sport.

The area was bustling with life. Cameramen were getting in place. The lighting illuminated the land but did little to make it welcoming.

Krista shuddered and rubbed her shoulders, looking around. She felt like she was being watched. The uneasy feeling followed her all the way to meeting with hair and make-up. Gregor stayed with her every step of the way like he promised. Even knowing that someone was out there and could be close by, he made her feel safe.

Right now, he was standing just off to her right, eyes scanning the perimeter of the land, watching everyone and everything. She wondered if he'd served in the military. His mannerisms reminded her of someone that had been. Even in this area, where only approved people could get through the gates, he was vigilant.

"You know you can go take a break and relax a little."

He planted his feet shoulder width apart and crossed his arms, pinning her with his ice-blue eyes. "I'm good."

"And obviously stubborn. Seriously, Gregor, I'm perfectly safe here. You can go do other things if you have to."

"I'm on the clock. I'll be right over there if you need me." He pointed to a bench under a mossy oak.

Krista shrugged. "Suit yourself. I've got work to do." She relaxed in the chair and let her makeup and hair team work their magic.

KRISTA WAS beautiful without makeup and he had a hard time keeping his eyes to himself whether she was in disguise or just getting out of bed. He wasn't afraid to admit she was a sight he could get used to. But when she emerged from the makeup chair, his breath caught in his throat. The woman was damn fine. His cock wanted to do a happy dance in his trousers.

Watching Krista at work was amazing. The girl could run in stilettos through the woods like a fucking champ. He'd break his legs if he attempted that.

His phone buzzed in his pocket and he checked the screen.

GOT SOME INFO FOR YOU.

· · ·

It was from Gunther. He glanced at the scene being filmed in front of him and deduced that Krista was in safe hands. He walked out to the gate and left the fenced in area so he wouldn't disrupt them. He didn't want Krista to scream any more than she had to. How she had a voice left at the end of the day, he had no idea. Either way it was impressive.

He dialed his brother's phone and waited for him to answer. "Magnuson."

"It's me. What'd you find out?"

"Hey, how's the shoot going?"

"You know how it is. Lots of stop and go."

"Yeah, not really, but I'll take your word for it." He chuckled. "I got a general area on your skin walker."

"Fuck. You know where?"

"It's not that easy. But it's safe to say he's hanging around the general area of the hotel. Could be in the hotel, but we can't pinpoint it down that closely."

"Not really what I want to hear. This job would be so much easier if he wasn't a skin walker. But he is, and it's making this beyond difficult." He ran his hands through his hair. A scream rent through the air and he whipped his head back to the gate, ready to pounce, before realizing it was Krista filming a scene.

"Everything okay?"

"Yeah, thanks for the info, Gunth. I've got to go."

"You sure? I thought I heard someone scream."

Gregor chuckled. "You did. Krista. She's working on a scene."

"Damn. She's got a set of lungs on her. You better not ever piss her off, little brother. She'll scream and the whole neighborhood will come running to help."

"You've got that right. She's perfected it for sure."

"Alright, man. Let me know if you need anything else."

His brother ended the call with a click.

Gregor needed to come up with a plan. If Thaddeus was watching Krista from the hotel, he'd have to be prepared for anything. And he had to work on getting her to see the depth of danger that she was in.

Right now, she just thought it was an overzealous fan. He wasn't sure how she'd react to finding out that it was a supernatural being.

He wasn't supposed to tell her. The whole purpose of The Guardians was to protect their world. Not to introduce humans to it.

He'd have to think about it. Right now, he had no idea how to draw Thaddeus out and get him to reveal himself. It was going to take some quick thinking on Gregor's part.

And as much as he didn't want to admit it, he was almost positive that he was going to have to use an unwitting Krista as a pawn.

AS THADDEUS TRUDGED through the marshy swampland known as Florida, he decided he was not a fan. The bugs were ridiculous. The cloying heat and humidity, unbearable.

The filming location was deep in the swamp and he had to be careful not to be seen. This wasn't a place that one would just stumble upon by accident. The production crew had chosen well.

He stayed back and listened. Watched as the muscle head left the gate to make a phone call. Thaddeus shrank further into the woods, hiding behind a huge oak tree, its branches hanging low to add extra coverage. He felt a sharp prick on his leg and caught himself before he swatted at whatever was feasting on his flesh.

He didn't want them to know he was here. He wanted to scope out the set for a few days.

Krista's scream echoed through the trees and he smiled. Such a sweet sound. He only wished he could see her face as she yelled. See her full, red lips open as the sound escaped her lungs.

He didn't want to hurt her. He just wanted her to believe.

In him.

In his world.

Why was that too much to ask?

The director yelled cut and everyone started talking at once, making enough noise to disguise any that he might make as he swatted away the red ants feasting on his legs. Painful little bastards.

Her bodyguard went back to the set and Thaddeus drew a sigh of relief. The man posed a problem, but nothing he couldn't handle. The guy couldn't be with Krista twenty-four-seven.

He was a patient man. He'd just wait for his chance.

They continued filming well into the night and it was after midnight when they finally called it a day.

He watched as everyone left, including Krista. She looked beautiful even after a long day of running and screaming. She hardly had a hair out of place.

After everyone left, he wandered over to the filming area. The fence had to be about 8 feet tall with metal anchors posted into the soft ground to keep it stable. He pushed against the wall and it hardly budged. Thankfully, it was sturdy enough for him to scale.

With a final glance around, he hopped up, grabbed the lip and pulled himself up and over. Inside, Krista's scent was everywhere. He inhaled deeply. Taking all of her in with a smile. He paced the perimeter of the set, familiarizing himself with the layout. Recording every detail to memory.

The makeup and hair station was set up in the far corner, and while he looked around he found the brush they used on Krista's hair., a few strands of red still caught in the bristles. He pocketed it and gave one last sweep of the area, before leaving, happy with his newfound souvenir.

CHAPTER TEN

"**I**'m starving." She swept a gaze over Gregor. He looked as refreshed and awake as if he'd just gotten out of bed and drank a full pot of coffee. "I hate these long filming days."

"I'll see what I can do about getting some food for you. If they're going to keep you there so late, they should make sure to have adequate provisions."

Adequate provisions? He talked odd at times. That sounded so old-fashioned. Like something her grandparents would have said. "Usually they do. I don't think they expected us to be there so late tonight." She swallowed and winced. Her throat was a little sore from all the screaming. "I need some tea and honey for my throat."

They arrived at his truck and he held open the passenger door while she climbed in. "I'll get you some."

"Is there anything open this late?" She looked out the window at the inky blackness of night. Maybe it was just their location, but it looked like they were in a dead zone.

Gravel spit out from the tires as Gregor pulled out of the parking lot. He activated the phone system on the steering wheel and called the hotel. Once room service was on the line, he barked off an order and before hanging up added "chamomile tea and honey."

"It's pretty late for room service. I'm surprised they even took your order."

They have staff on call at all times for us while we're here. It was arranged before we arrived."

"Nice. That could come in handy."

He glanced at her out of the corner of his eye. "You plan on a lot of late nights?"

She shrugged. "Maybe." She extended her arms and stretched, feeling the muscles in her back loosen. "You never know."

BACK IN THEIR suite with the room service he'd ordered spread over the kitchen counter, Krista was sipping wine and chatting away, only taking the occasional break to catch her breath and scroll through her phone.

She'd changed into an off the shoulder gray sweatshirt and black leggings and tied her red hair into a messy bun. A few rogue strands framed her face. He wanted to reach out and tuck them behind her ear. Her beauty was getting harder to ignore the more time he spent with her.

He could go for some whiskey right about now. So, he opened the fridge and studied the items inside. Milk, soda, water, wine. Nothing stronger.

Krista sidled up next to him and reached over to grab another wine glass.

"Here." She poured some pinot into the glass and handed it to him. "Take it." She insisted when he didn't accept her offering.

"I'm on the clock."

"Yeah, and you work for me. Sooo," she drawled out the word, "technically, you need to do as I say. And I say have a glass of damn wine." She stuck out her bottom lip in a sexy pout. She was probably going for sad, but it was sexy. So. Fucking. Sexy.

She grasped his hand and shoved the wine bottle into it. "Come on. I hate drinking alone."

Wine was no whiskey, but who was he to tell her no? He accepted the glass and clinked the edge to hers and lifted it up. "Cheers." He said before taking a long sip.

"See? That wasn't so hard, was it?"

If she only knew how hard it really was...

"For tonight only. Because it's been a long day. Tomorrow we're back to strictly business."

She dismissed that statement with a wave of her hand. "We'll see about that." She finished the last sip and reached for the bottle, but Gregor beat her to it and refilled her glass. "How long have you lived in the states?" She asked.

The question came out of the blue.

"Your accent is faint, but it's still there."

He couldn't tell her the truth. She'd probably move to have him committed. What would be an acceptable answer? "Since my teens." Gregor answered. "I haven't lived there for a long time."

"Scotland is on my bucket list of places to visit."

He'd love to take her there. Show her his ancestral home. He wondered what she'd think of it. But stopped that train of thought before it went off the rails. There was no she and him. There couldn't be.

This was strictly business.

"Hey," she jumped off the kitchen stool. "You want to listen to some music? Doesn't matter. I want to listen to music. So, we're going to." She disappeared down the hall and returned a minute later with a small portable speaker.

"You carry that wherever you go?"

"When I'm traveling yes. Music is life. And the speaker on my phone doesn't sound good. This little baby," she held up the small cube, "packs a punch." She powered it on and opened her music application on her phone, hitting play. Pop music filled the suite. A song Gregor was unfamiliar with.

Krista, apparently knew it well. She grabbed her wine glass off the counter and held it up to him in salute, and took a sip before closing her eyes and swaying her hips. She whipped her head around, causing her bun to loosen and her hair begin to fall. She reached back and let it free from the elastic loosely holding it. Shaking her head back and forth to free it fully.

Gregor watched, mesmerized. The wine was loosening her up. Not that she was uptight before. Just more controlled. But now, with just the two of them and the wine flowing freely, she was letting her guard down.

Was it a sign she was becoming more comfortable with having him around? He felt a tinge of happiness begin to spread in his chest.

She held her hand out. "Come dance with me."

He shook his head. "I haven't had nearly enough liquor for that. I'm not a dancer."

She brushed his remark off. "That doesn't matter. It's just us. Who's going to see?"

You.

That was an embarrassment he'd rather avoid. But she was making it difficult to deny her. She came close, definitely ignoring his personal boundaries. He lost it when she shimmied in front of him.

Who knew leggings and a baggy sweatshirt could be such a turn-on? She took another sip of wine before setting the glass on the counter and grabbed his hand, pulling him to the open space between the suite's living room and kitchen. Her touch was electric. Shooting bolts of friction up his arm and straight to his cock.

He chugged his wine and emptied the glass. Then stuck it on the side table by the sofa.

Fine. He was all in.

But just for tonight.

She shot him a wicked smile that hinted at devilish things and his mind was swamped with all things sexual. With his hand still in hers, she rocked it back and forth, moving to the rhythm of the music. Letting the beat overtake her.

"Gregor."

"Hmmm?"

"Don't make me do all the work. Move that big body of yours."

He grasped her hips and pulled her close. She yelped in surprise. "Oh, I'm willing to do the work." Her lips parted and all he wanted to do was claim her mouth with his. He was treading in very dangerous water.

His brain kept telling him that's not what he was here for. It's a job. It's a job.

It's. A. Job. Kept running through his mind, but his body had other intentions.

He wanted her.

Bad.

Oh, so bad.

When she looked at him, challenge running rampant in the caramel depths of her eyes, the battle was lost.

The taste of her lips on his was heavenly. If he believed in the mythical place, he imagined that's where he'd find Krista.

She sighed and melted against him. The warmth of her body heating his.

Their tongues played a tentative dance before giving up the fight and committing fully to the earth-shattering kiss.

This was where he wanted to be. Where he needed to be. In this beautiful woman's arms.

And then reality invaded and broke the magical moment.

He tore his mouth away from hers. Her lips swollen from their kiss, her eyes hooded.

His cock, hard and ready, tried to punch through his pants to get at the tasty morsel being offered in front of him.

"Krista..." he let his voice trail off.

She took a step back, clasping her hands in front of her. She opened her mouth to say something, but clamped it shut. Right before turning and walking briskly to her room. The slamming door the perfect ending to this screwed up night.

THE NEXT DAY on the set the tension was multiplied. It hung heavy in the air. Gregor hadn't said a word to her on the drive over. Probably because she shut him down when she'd woken up this morning and gone out for coffee.

They crossed the line last night and they both knew it.

But, damn.

It was a line she'd so enjoyed crossing. Underneath that hard exterior that man was all warm skin, gentle hands and an amazing mouth.

Just thinking about it caused her to shudder in delight.

But, they shouldn't have kissed. It was the worst possible scenario for both of them. Her track record sucked. Her security were supposedly off limits. So, why was she was always attracted to them? She was going to tell Jessica and Natalie that from here on out, all her security team needed to be unattractive. She definitely had a type, and Gregor fit it perfectly.

"Krista?" The director called to her. "You ready?"

She stood and rubbed her hands together. Enough about

men. She had a job to do. Just like Gregor. Unfortunately for her, his job didn't include warming her bed at night. No matter how much she wanted him too.

An assistant approached her and dabbed some powder on her cheeks. The humidity made her skin so oily it was disgusting. Every few minutes she needed a touch up to make sure her face wasn't shining like a beacon.

The assistant, a male, seemed to linger a little too long. It struck Krista as odd. She wasn't sure why and couldn't point to anything in particular, but usually they just did a quick brush of powder and went on their way. This man stayed, looking deep into her eyes.

Instinctively, she looked for Gregor. He was sitting on the bench checking his messages on his phone. He looked up, was that concern marring his handsome features? He stood and the assistant scurried away. Even he knew not to mess with Gregor.

His long strides closed the distance between them quickly. "Everything going okay?" He scanned the clearing as he waited for her reply. He was all business. Evidently, he was still put off by last night.

She wasn't normally a suspicious person, but knowing she had a stalker out there running loose had her nerves on edge. "It's nothing."

He raised a honey-colored brow in question.

She shook her head. "I think I'm just nervous with everything that's going on."

He gave her a curt nod before heading over to one of the refreshment stations to get a bottle of water.

Again, Krista was amazed by how turned on she could be by watching a man drink from a water bottle.

She had to get herself together.

She turned to head over to the director. She had lines to go over.

THADDEUS WAS PRETTY SURE the iron mountain Krista had hired as her security was a Guardian. Everywhere she went, he was right there.

He was also pretty sure protecting her wasn't the only thing on the oaf's mind. The way he looked at her, those ice blue eyes tingeing with blue flames every time he set his sight on her beauty.

Black anger clouded his vision. He had to play this smart and stay off the Guardian's radar. He thought he'd been caught earlier when he'd freshened up Krista's makeup. He didn't know a thing about cosmetics. But posing as the assistant allowed him to get closer to Krista than he'd ever been before. Even closer than in the club.

He touched her. Soft skin. She smelled like flowers.

He wanted to shout at her to show her what she was missing even though it was laid out right before her.

But that was something he wanted to do when it was just the two of them. A lot of planning was needed to pull that off.

But he'd do it.

Krista Wallingford would soon see that it wasn't only humans that roamed this earth.

CHAPTER ELEVEN

"**T**hat's a wrap!" Rogan bellowed into the megaphone. "Great job, everyone!"

Krista breathed a sigh of relief. "Thank God," she muttered under her breath. Now that the shoot was done, she could head back to L.A. and get out of this dreadful humidity.

And away from Gregor Magnuson.

The past two weeks had been torture. She and Gregor just going through the motions. Being civil. Being friendly. It was making her crazy.

He was so cold. Acting all professional. He hadn't so much as had a sip of wine or alcohol since the night they'd kissed.

And he definitely had not kissed her again.

And that pissed her off.

She knew it shouldn't. But, damn. She wanted him to kiss her again.

"Krista," Rogan called out as he jogged up to her. "I know this wasn't your favorite location, but you did great. We might have to call you back for a couple of scenes, but we won't know until editing."

She smiled. "As long as I can redo them in Cali, I'll be fine."

"I'm sure we can make it work. Have a safe trip home. I'll be in touch."

"Ready?" Gregor asked from behind her.

"Geesh! Stop creeping up on me like that." She grumbled. For a huge guy, he was eerily quiet. And sneaky. If he wasn't so big, he'd make a great cat burglar.

He ignored her. "I'll grab your bag and we can head back to the hotel."

"Gregor," he turned, and she paused. She didn't know what to say. She was so tired of this weird charade they were playing.

"Do you need something?"

"Never mind," she mumbled and pushed past him. She could get her own damn bag.

MUSIC FILLED the cab of the SUV. Lately, Krista had perfected the art of the cold shoulder. It hurt, but he'd be damned if he'd let her know it bothered him.

All things considered, this was the best possible outcome. If they didn't talk to each other, there was no risk of blurring the lines between professional and personal.

He approached a slow-moving car and swore before hitting his blinker and mashing the gas pedal to get around the sedan, the elderly woman who could just barely able to see over the top of the steering wheel as she drove without a care in the world on who she inconvenienced.

"In a rush to get home, I see." Krista smirked. Her ruby red lips full and beautiful.

"Some people need to stay off the road when they have no business driving."

"That's harsh."

"But the truth."

She crossed her arms, the gesture pushing up her ample breasts, the pale skin peeking out of her v-neck tee shirt. He inhaled sharply. There was no way he could let her go home without trying to see if there was something there.

He was pretty sure she felt it, too.

Plus, Thaddeus was still out there somewhere.

She wouldn't be safe until he was sent back to the Other-world. The Council expected Gregor to deliver Thaddeus to them on the equivalent of a silver platter and he wouldn't get paid until he did.

"Well, you won't have to deal with the annoying drivers much longer."

"That's where you're wrong." He flipped his blinker on and eased into the turning lane, waiting for the light to turn green. "Your stalker is still out there and as long as he is, you and I won't be parting ways."

She harrumphed, slouching in her seat. "We'll see about that."

The hotel came into view and he pulled into the lot, circling until he found a spot and backed in. Surprisingly, Krista stayed put until he came around to her side and opened the door, then helped her out.

His hand burned at her touch as she placed her palm in his. Her gaze met his for the briefest of moments before she stepped out of the SUV and started toward the hotel lobby. The connection was broken too soon for his liking.

He wanted them to clear the air. To stop being so awkward around each other. Something had to give. He followed her closely, ushering her inside and onto the elevator.

They rode in silence, listening to the ding as each floor ticked by before the doors slid open on their floor.

"I can talk to Natalie and let her know that your job is done." She dropped her purse on the nearest chair once they entered their suite and went straight to the fridge, pulling out a bottle of chardonnay. "Do you want a glass?"

He shook his head. What he wanted was her. Not a glass of wine. Not to be sent on his way. Not to be dismissed. He wanted her. In his bed. In his life.

"I'm going to grab a quick shower. Then we can figure out what you want to do for dinner." He left her rummaging through the drawer, searching for the corkscrew. He should be a gentleman and open the bottle for her, but if he got any closer, he feared he'd wrap her in his arms and kiss the breath right out of her.

WHY THE HELL was this bottle being so difficult to open? She blew the hair out of her face with an exasperated breath and stuck the bottle in the sink.

Sitting at the bar, she waited for Gregor to finish his shower, tapping her fingers against the cold stone. Visions of his golden skin, naked, just in the other room, water trickling down over his chest, his pecs, his rock-hard abs, down to his rock hard... "Oh my *God*." She muttered, disgusted with herself for falling into the same trap she'd been warned about relentlessly.

"You know, the problem is you're drinking wine." Gregor said from behind her. Damn, that man was quiet when he wanted to be. "What you need is some good 'ol whisky."

With his hair still damp from the shower, Krista found him more attractive than before, if that was even possible.

She tried to not concentrate on how much she wanted to feel his hands on her skin. All over her body.

"Shows how much you know. I'm not having wine."

He ambled over to the sink and lifted the bottle she'd unceremoniously left there and examined it. "Having difficulties?" He brought it over to the bar and reached for the cork screw. "Truly, whisky would be so much better than wine. And easier."

Krista looked around. "Yeah, but I don't see any here, so wine it is. Whether you like it or not." She pushed a stemmed glass toward him, knowing he'd have the bottle uncorked in no time.

And like a Boy Scout, he did. He poured her a glass and set the bottle down.

"Nothing for you? Really, Gregor, you can have a drink."

He paused, seeming to think about her suggestion and shook his head. "If I recall, the last time I ventured a drink or two, we stopped talking for an unreasonable amount of time. Seeing how I still have a job to do and since I quite like talking to you, I'm going to pass."

Krista lifted her glass in a mock cheer. "Suit yourself. I'm going to indulge." She snagged the bottle off the counter and carried it and her glass into the living room and settled on the couch, sinking into the cushions before tucking her feet under her.

When he sat down beside her, with his massive frame weighing the cushions down, she tried to hide her smile. She ridiculously felt like she'd just won the lottery. She dipped her head, her hair falling like a curtain in front of her face. Through the fringe, she glanced at him, watching him cast a furtive glance her way.

With a flick of her wrist, she tucked her hair behind her ear and leaned forward to snatch the remote. "Anything in particular you want to watch?"

He remained silent and just watched her. His ice-blue eyes darkening to a murky gray. Was it desire that flickered there? Heat pooled between her legs.

As if in slow motion, Gregor reached over to her, cupping the back of her head, drawing her close before capturing her lips. The heat of his mouth claimed hers and with a soft sigh, she relented, giving him the full access he wordlessly requested. She dropped the remote with a loud clatter, startling them both.

He laughed. A low, deep rumble. "I'll take that." He took the wine glass from her hand and placed it carefully toward the center of the table before turning his full attention back to her. A feral look in his eyes. "In answer to your question, I want to watch you."

She swallowed hard. "Me?" Her voice came out barely a whisper that sounded husky even to her own ears.

"Mmhmm." He trailed kisses along her jawline, nuzzling her neck before kissing his way to her ear and sucking gently on the lobe.

She gasped.

"I want you, Krista. I've wanted you since the moment I picked you up at the airport." He captured her mouth in a deep kiss and she melted into him. The warmth of his body seeping into hers, enveloping her in a security blanket in which she'd never felt safer.

For the first time in a long time, she didn't think about her stalker. The danger that she may be in. Just the here and now. This beautiful moment that she and Gregor were sharing. She wanted him, mind, body and soul.

He stood and brought her with him, gently tugging on her hand, pulling her towards the bedrooms. Which one would they enter? To her, it didn't matter. The result was going to be the same.

Tonight, Gregor Magnuson would claim her as his.

CHAPTER TWELVE

K rista stood in front of his bed, looking up at him. Her eyes warm and welcoming. He knew he should stop. Should march her out the door and leave her in her own room. Alone.

But, damn. One glance from her chocolate brown eyes, and he was done.

He wasn't lying when he told her he wanted her from the first moment he saw her. You couldn't fight fate. He'd learned that over his many years walking this earth.

An uneasiness started wrangling its way into his head. Could he do this? Take her when he hadn't been upfront about who he really was? She had no idea he wasn't fully human. How would she react? He should tell her. But he'd made a vow.

Humans were not to know they existed. It's why the Guardians were born. To keep that secret safe.

She reached out and ran a small hand down his chest. He grasped it, closing his eyes, and bringing it to his lips, placing a kiss on the tip of each polished nail.

"Gregor..." her voice trailed off as he pulled her close. The lengths of their bodies connecting, comprising a mold as if they'd been made for each other.

You can't fight fate.

That line was going to be his new motto when he was with Krista. He'd come clean to her, but now wasn't the time.

She stood on her tip toes, wrapping her arms around the back of his neck. "I want you, Gregor Magnuson."

Gods above, she was so confident. And he felt like a teenaged boy sleeping with a girl for the very first time. "I'm not sure we should..."

She kissed him. Soft, gentle. "You need to finish what you started." She nipped at his bottom lip. A gesture that had all his blood shooting straight to his cock. He groaned.

"This is a professional relationship." He grasped for words. For reasons why they shouldn't go any further.

And failed miserably.

"It still can be." Her hands dropped to his waist, her fingers playing with the hem of his shirt, as she lifted the soft material and bent, placing soft kisses on his chest, his pecs. Her hot mouth sucked on his nipple as she pushed the material further up to his shoulders.

"Jesus." He gasped, reaching for the restricting material and pulling it over his head, discarding it on the floor. He brought her head up and dipped his to meet her mouth, then stole a soul-stealing kiss that left him as hard as if he were in gargoyle form.

He needed to see her. To touch her. Needed her naked in front of him. He lifted her shirt and with a flick of his wrist it pooled on the floor beside his.

Her breasts spilled over the black lace demi-bra she wore. He hissed and made quick work of the sexy obstruction.

Krista's eyes widened, a seductive smile forming her mouth, before she bent and slowly drew her pants down, bringing her panties with them. She stepped out of them, leaving her standing in front of him.

Naked.

Beautiful.

He captured her mouth again. Passion putting force into the kiss.

With their lips still locked, Gregor pushed her back onto the bed. She sat, and breaking the kiss, scooted toward the middle, making room for him to join her.

He stood for a moment, drinking in the sight of her. "You're beautiful."

Her cheeks flushed. Hell, her whole body was flushed, the skin rosy pink. Holding out her arms, she smiled and it was all the invitation he needed. He dropped his sweats and felt a swell of pride at the widening of her eyes when she saw his hardened cock.

Sliding on the bed, he wrapped her in his arms, burying his face in her neck, inhaling the sweet smell of her flowery perfume. The sensual musk of her skin. It was enough to send him over the edge.

Rolling on top of her, he shifted her leg, bringing her knee up to his hip, holding it there while he trailed soft kisses along her collarbone.

"Are you sure this is what you want?" He whispered. He'd stop if she said no. It would be one of the most difficult things he'd ever done though, because the only thing he could think of right now was sinking his hardness into her core until she screamed his name to the Gods.

But he had integrity.

He'd stop.

She hissed when he nipped at the sensitive flesh at her nape. "I'm sure."

Thank the fucking stars above.

He lifted himself up onto his elbows and concentrated

his attention on her breasts, the creamy globes soft to his touch, her nipples hardening as he brushed his lips over each one. His tongue darted out to have a taste and her low moan of pleasure shot vibrations straight to his cock.

He blew a breath of air over the wet nipple making her buck her hips. He smiled and sucked it all the way into his mouth, and her hands flew to his head. If he had any length to his hair, she would've fisted her hands in it.

Slowly, he kissed his way down to her navel, then kept going. Drinking in the scent of her. Reveling in the feel of her.

As Gregor's mouth met with her core, she gasped, instinctively closing her legs. He chuckled and nudged her legs further apart, pushing up under her thighs, allowing him full access to all she had to offer. His tongue swept against her folds, and her sweet taste filled his mouth, making him mad with desire.

Her moans filling him with pride.

She writhed beneath him and he stilled her with a heavy arm. He wasn't finished tasting her yet.

Wasn't sure he ever would be.

Krista's hands grasped at his shoulders, tugging at him, pushing him away one minute, then pulling him back the next. He felt her need.

Could feel it in the urgency of her touch. In the intensity of her moans.

And he smiled in victory.

With a final kiss to her core, he slid up her body. She kissed him deeply. His cock twitched, knowing she could taste herself on his tongue.

So. Fucking. Hot.

"I need to be in you."

"Yes..." she breathed, her voice husky.

He positioned himself, ready to claim her wholly when she pushed him back.

"Wait!"

Hips midair, he looked at her, concern flooded through him. "What's wrong?" He tried to tamp down the feeling of disappointment that she didn't want this to happen.

"We need protection."

"What?" Gregor asked, confused. "You know I'll never let anything happen to you."

She smacked him in the chest. "Not that." Her eyes widened. "A condom."

Relief washed over him. "Of course." He bent and kissed her forehead before reaching into the nightstand drawer and pulling out a foil packet.

"Let me." She took the condom from him and tore it open with her teeth then pulled it from its packaging. She kissed him as her hand wrapped around his cock.

His breath caught as she slowly covered his shaft, and it took all his power not to come right then and there. "If you don't hurry, this is going to be over with very quickly." He raised his brows. "If you know what I'm saying."

She smiled seductively. And once she'd finished tormenting him, he reached down and grabbed her hands and brought them up over her head as he guided his cock to her opening.

She was ready for him.

So wet.

He thrust into her. Filling her. Feeling her take him in, adjusting to his size, and because she felt so damn good, he let out a moan to match hers.

And then he stilled. Afraid if he moved, he'd be done.

She squirmed under him. Rocking her hips.

It was all he could take. He drew himself almost all the way out before driving back in deep. Repeatedly. His thrusts were urgent. His hips thrusting. He could hear his blood pounding in his ears.

Through a haze of passion, he could hear Krista calling out his name. It was the hottest thing he'd ever heard. And when her pussy clamped down on his cock, he quickened his pace, wanting to climax with her. She was so damn sexy. He wanted to dominate her. Make her his. And by the urgency of her touch as she held onto him, she was getting close.

"Gregor!" She yelled and shuddered beneath him, her breath coming in short gasps and her nails biting into his skin as her body hit its breaking point.

He followed right behind her. Growling out his climax as his cock swelled inside her as he came. Spurts of come spilling forth with his final thrusts.

Breathing ragged, he dropped his face to her neck and nipped at the skin just below her throat. No other woman compared to the utter bliss he'd just felt in Krista's arms

Not wanting the moment to end, he rolled onto his back, bringing her with him. He made quick work of the condom and then settled her on his heaving chest.

He buried his hands in her hair, massaging her scalp as they both came down from their bliss.

THE NEXT MORNING, Krista woke, still in Gregor's bed, his muscled arm draped over her stomach. She studied his sleeping form. The man was beautiful.

And sexy.

And one hell of a lover.

Last night, when she'd kissed his nipples, just the thought sending a delicious shiver through her, she'd noticed the huge, Celtic-style tattoo on his right pec. She'd been too preoccupied to pay it much attention then, but now, in the early light of morning with him sleeping so peacefully, she studied the intricate artwork. It was a knot-work circle. Gingerly, she traced her fingers along the curvy lines.

Their night together had been amazing, but it was over now, so she carefully extracted herself from Gregor's grasp, being careful not to wake him. Quietly, she gathered her clothes and winced at the soreness between her thighs. It was a pleasurable pain. One she hadn't felt in a really long time. If ever, now that she thought about it.

Making her way to her own room, she tossed her clothes in the corner, turned on the hot water and brushed her teeth while she waited for stem to fill the room.

She needed a hot shower. A bath would be better, but she there was no time. They needed to get packed and head to the airport.

As the water poured over her body, soothing her aches and pains, regret overwhelmed her. Not because of last night. But because it couldn't last. She had to head back to California. And Gregor would go back to wherever it was he was from.

Her stalker hadn't made an appearance in a couple of weeks and she was sure that he'd moved on to another target.

She hoped so.

Her mind wandered to the night before. They had made love two more times throughout the night. Hot, steamy, passionate sex. She couldn't remember the last time she'd lost herself in someone so completely.

Gregor's scent was still on her skin, and she didn't want to wash it away.

She wanted to hold him close to her heart forever, to remember their perfect night and commit his scent to memory. She was glad he was still sleeping when she woke up, because she didn't want it to be awkward and spoil the moment. Yet, she didn't need to worry because he hadn't moved a muscle, not even when she got out of bed. He was always so alert. She smiled. Maybe she'd managed to finally exhaust the man.

A noise from the kitchen caught her ear and she turned off the water, thinking Gregor must've woken up.

She quickly dried off and dressed, but when she stepped out of her room and into the kitchen, it was empty.

Knock. Knock.

Did he accidentally lock himself out of the room? Odd. That would be completely out of character for him.

Opening the door to let Gregor in, she joked with him, "I don't believe--" Her words were cut short when the figure standing at the door plunged a needle into the side of her neck. "Ow!" Within seconds her world turned blurry before disappearing into an inky darkness.

KRISTA WOKE up in an unfamiliar room and looked around.

Where was she?

The room was small, with gray walls and no windows. A ceiling fan whirred above the double bed she was laying on, but the breeze it offered was hardly any defense against the humidity that hung heavy in the air.

Wherever she was, she didn't think central air was included.

She tried to swing her legs over the side of the bed, but they felt so heavy and her movements were slow.

What the hell happened?

Pain exploded in her head as she sat upright. She massaged her temples, as she took in her surroundings.

This definitely wasn't the suite she shared with Gregor. *Gregor!* Where was he? Her body trembled and she fought it. She needed to pull it together. What the hell was going on?

A small nightstand beside the bed held a glass filled with clear liquid. Water? Maybe. Though she wasn't going to drink it and find out. She didn't dare. Her mind was already foggy. Something was wrong. Really wrong. She felt like she'd been drugged. How?

She tried to clear the cobwebs from her memory to figure out what happened.

The last thing she remembered was -- what? She blew out an exasperated breath. She couldn't remember.

Carefully, she stood, testing her legs to make sure they wouldn't give out on her. She was unsteady on her feet, and her limbs tingled, but she was able to put one foot in front of the other without falling. She said a silent prayer. Other than the bed and the nightstand, there was nothing else in the room. Only one door, which had to lead out. Slowly, she made her way to it, using the wall to help keep her steady.

She turned the knob and pulled.

Nothing.

It was locked. Her heart sunk and panic started to settle in now that her mind was beginning to clear.

She pulled harder on the handle to no avail.

She studied the room, looking for something, anything she could use as a weapon.

There was nothing.

Reaching in her back pocket for her phone, she wasn't surprised to find it empty.

Of course, whoever had locked her in here would've taken it.

She wracked her brain. Wished she could remember.

Was it her stalker?

Her stomach lurched.

How?

How was he able to get through Gregor?

She tugged and tugged on the door, but it wouldn't open.

Tears sprouted in her eyes. Frantic, she banged on the door. "Hello?" She yelled. "Help!"

She kept hitting the door until her knuckles were red and split and her palms were bloody. No one came. She wasn't sure she if she was thankful for that or if she wanted someone to open it so she could see who it was that that locked her in here.

Oh God. What would Gregor think? Would he think she just left him? Like before. He must be flipping out. What if he didn't realize she was gone. No. Of course he'd notice. But, how long had she been here? Hours? Days? She had no idea. And no way to tell.

Krista slumped to the floor, cradled her head in her bloodied hands, and let her tears flow freely, the drops soaking the worn carpet. Sobs wracked her body. She wanted out of this place. She didn't know what she was doing here, anyway.

If the person wanted money, they were going about it the wrong way.

CHAPTER THIRTEEN

The shrill caw of a crow awakened Gregor from the deepest sleep he'd had in years, well, outside of his gargoyle form. Decades, even.

Krista's scent was heavy in the air, enticing him, making him stand at attention, but a stretch of his arm proved that he was alone in his bed. Krista was gone.

He groaned, wishing she had stayed in his bed. He wanted nothing more than to bury himself deep inside her again.

His cock jerked at the thought, and he went to grasp his shaft, the urge to stroke himself to relief strong. But it wouldn't be satisfying. Not after Krista.

Nothing could live up to the feeling of her tight wetness pulling him deeper into her depths.

"Gods." He couldn't stop thinking about the previous night. He shuddered knowing they shouldn't have crossed that line. *He* shouldn't have crossed that line. If history repeated itself, the future didn't bode well.

He refused to believe that.

Was it worth the risk?

Gregor thought of Krista writhing in passion beneath him, her lips full and swollen from his kisses. Hell yes, it had been worth it.

Every. Fucking. Second.

Rubbing his face with his palms to wake himself up, he figured it was time to get out of bed and do something productive. The suite was quiet. Maybe Krista had gone to sleep in her own bed. He was amazed he hadn't heard her get up.

Apparently when he finally fell asleep last night he was well sated.

Dead to the world.

Did she regret their time together? Regret giving in to what they both were feeling but didn't want to admit?

Anxious to see Krista, he quickly showered and dressed and made his way to the kitchen to start the coffee. Once it was ready, he knocked on her bedroom door. The door wasn't latched and swung open from his tap.

She wasn't in bed. "Krista?" He entered the room and looked around. It was empty. Fear crept into his veins. He checked the bathroom. No sign of Krista in there either. He threw the coffee cup he was holding into the sink, ignoring the shattering of glass as he ran out of the room.

Krista was nowhere to be found. "Fuck! "He grabbed his keys and jerked the door open. The scents of Krista and Thaddeus mingled together assaulted his nose while images of Katherine flooded his mind.

He failed Krista. The same way he failed Katherine. "Not this time." He spat. "Not again." He grabbed his keys and ran out into the lot. Finding Krista the only thing on his mind.

"Hold on, baby."

THE SOUND of metal scraping against metal caught Krista's attention from where she sat on the floor in the corner furthest from the door. Though her eyes swollen from crying, she focused on the knob as it turned and the door slowly opened.

Her breath hitched as a man entered the room. She hugged herself tighter, a defense that would do nothing to protect her.

He looked familiar, and she tried to remember where she'd seen him before, as she sat silently, afraid to move. Afraid to do anything.

He approached her, a grotesque sneer stretched across his face.

Krista shrank back, her body trembling. "It's you." Recognition dawned as she studied him. "You worked with the film crew."

He sat on the edge of the bed, elbows on his knees, the mattress creaking under his weight. "You remember when you gave that interview? The one where you said you don't believe in any of the things in your movies?" He asked, ignoring her question.

Krista shrugged. "I don't know. It's something I say often." Her voice barely above a whisper.

"How can you not see what is right in front of you? A whole world is presented to you and you refuse to acknowledge it."

She had no idea what he was talking about. The guy was obviously delusional. How he hid his craziness from everyone was beyond her. Her body began to tremble again and she hated it. Her body was betraying her. Instead of showing strength she was showing weakness. Not the best way to react toward a deranged person.

He leaned in close, his hot breath blowing in her face,

making her gag. But his rancid breath wasn't what caught her attention. His eyes did. They were odd, not like she remembered, but she really hadn't paid a whole lot of attention to him.

"We are all around you humans. Walking among you. Only you deny it." He spat.

What the hell was he talking about? This guy was insane. Loony bin insane. Krista's fear heightened. How could she reason with someone who doesn't understand logic?

She wasn't sure if she should placate him or talk him down from the ledge, because everything coming out of his mouth was complete nonsense. *You humans?* Hello? Look in the mirror much?

His eyes swept over her and she actually felt his disdain. His leer was sinister, and just like that, her fear was back. That hopeful feeling she had briefly experienced was gone.

"Why am I here?" She demanded, trying not to let fear show in her voice, wanting him to think he didn't have her scared out of her mind. Not an easy feat, but she was trying.

He ignored her question, stood and began pacing the short length of the room. He stopped abruptly in front of her and bent down, his face level with hers. "I want you to see me!" Spittle sprayed her face as he spoke. She looked away, wishing the wall would open up and swallow her.

"Please, let me go. I promise I won't tell anyone." She begged, eyeing him warily.

His head fell back in maniacal laughter. "I'm not worried about you saying anything. Your human laws mean nothing to me."

Okay, the guy was truly off his rocker.

"Once you see me for who I really am, you'll understand. Our worlds will be one and we'll be happy."

"I don't understand. I'm sorry." She needed to get the hell

out of this room. The man in front of her was certifiable. She tried to think of a way to diffuse the situation. What was it that everyone said? Try to make friends with your captor. Get them talking. Make them feel at ease.

She could do that. She took a deep, shuddering breath. She was an actress. Surely, she could convince him that she was sincerely interested in what he had to say.

"Tell me more about your world," she said quietly.

His eyes lit up, and his persona completely changed. He dropped to the floor, stretching his legs out and leaned back against the bed. "You'll love it. The otherworld is an amazing place."

What the hell?

"It can be boring and repetitive at times," he continued. "Eternity is forever so you can't expect it to be exciting all the time."

The way he talked reminded Krista of someone brainwashed by a cult. He was saying such odd things. She would have to gain his trust to get out of here. So, she acted interested and waited for him to tell her more, no matter how outrageous it all sounded.

"Tell me why you don't believe in the supernatural?"

Krista wrestled with her answer. Lying might appease him. Or piss him off. Telling him the truth might do the same.

"Why do you think it's not real?" He asked, spittle spraying her face.

She blanched. "I don't know. In my movies, everything is manufactured. It takes the realness of it away."

"What if I could prove it to you?" His intense look frightened her even more.

"Prove what?" She didn't like where this conversation was heading. He was sending out a really creepy vibe.

"That the supernatural exists." He smiled. "Would that change your mind?"

"Yes," she said slowly. "It's hard to deny what's right in front of you."

He clapped loudly. "Exactly! That's what I've been trying to tell you. We are right here." He tapped his chest for emphasis.

She had no idea what he was going to do.

"We can be happy together. I'm sure of it. Once you know." He grabbed her hands and held tight. She tried to pull them way, but he had a vice-like grip on her. "Look at me."

She looked up at him and then, his face started to change. What the fuck was happening? He changed into another person. She pulled with all the strength she could muster and yanked her hands out of his grasp and scrambled to her feet.

"Stay away from me!"

"Krista. Don't be scared. It's still me. Look."

Shaking her head, she refused.

"Look at me!" He bellowed.

Her head shot up, body quaking in fear. What the hell was going on? Because right now, to her disbelief, his face was back to being the man from the film crew. She had to be seeing things. Or whatever he had drugged her with was still affecting her. There was no telling what he might do to her. She had to get the hell away from him.

Now.

Her eyes darted to the door. He wasn't near it. She could make a run for it.

Before she could let her fear change her mind, she bolted and pulled on the door handle, crying in relief when it opened. She ran into the hallway, but it was nothing but doors. She tried the first one she came to. Locked.

She tried the next.

Locked.

Tears streamed down her cheeks. She needed to get out of here. Whatever mind game he was playing with her was fucked up. It had to be the drugs he'd given her to get her here in the first place.

She kept trying the doors to no avail. She heard footsteps behind her and knew that she would have to fight. She should've listened to Gregor all those times he was talked to her about how to defend herself. He kept trying to tell her even after she explained she'd never have a need. That's what she had him around for.

God, she wished he was here. She spun and her captor was behind her.

Watching her.

"Leave me the fuck alone."

He clucked his tongue. "Now, Krista. Is that anyway to treat the person you're going to spend the rest of your life with?" His face split in a gruesome smile.

"You're crazy."

"Perhaps." He reached out and stroked her hair.

She slapped his hand away. "Don't touch me." She tried to run, but he boxed her in, bracing his hands against the wall on each side of her. She screamed. Loud, ear-piercing screams that she hoped would alert someone to her captivity.

"Stop that!"

She screamed louder.

"Stop screaming!" He grasped her shoulders and shook her, but she kept screaming. Someone had to hear her.

And then he slammed her head into the wall. Hard. She was dazed but kept screaming. When he slammed her again, everything went black.

GREGOR SPED over to the police station to meet his brother, not caring about how many laws he broke on the way.

He couldn't believe he'd let his guard down.

"Dammit!" He beat the steering wheel with his fist. This was the reason he didn't get involved with the people he was supposed to protect.

If he hadn't let his guard down, Krista would be with him right now.

There's no way Thaddeus would've gotten into the suite, let alone near enough to Krista to lay a hand on her.

If he hurt one hair on her beautiful head. Gods, help him. He was going to fucking kill that skin walker. Superior Council be damned. He would make sure Thaddeus wouldn't be a problem for anyone ever again.

His heart hurt. He didn't want to admit it to her. He loved her. He should've told her.

What was she thinking now? She must be scared to death. He'd let her down.

He couldn't even imagine the disappointment she must be feeling.

He completely failed her.

Trees whizzed by in a blur as he sped down the road. Gunther's voice held a note of surprise when he'd told him about Krista being gone as he'd run out of the hotel. Gregor kept his personal life private. He sure as Hell didn't share that information with his brother. But as he explained what happened, he couldn't help the crack in his voice. All he could think about was Krista's safety. And how he wished he'd told her how he truly felt.

He vowed to tell her once he got her back. And he would get her back. No matter what it took.

Ahead, cars were at a standstill. Gregor had to mash the brake pedal into the floor to stop from slamming into the cars in front of him.

Great. Now what? He didn't have time for this shit.

Traffic was stopped going on the North and South sides, and as he looked further down the highway he saw nothing but the equivalent of a parking lot. Why the hell hadn't he had his brother meet him at the suite? He was wasting precious time trying to do everything himself.

His relationship with Krista was affecting his thought process. With anyone else, this was a mistake he wouldn't have made.

Sirens blared in the distance. They were going to have a hell of a time trying to get through this mess, and since the lanes were blocked they were going to have to use the grassy median to get there.

In his rearview mirror he saw the police SUV and an ambulance approach and then slow down rapidly. He maneuvered his truck toward the middle to try to give them some space in the breakdown lane, but there wasn't much room.

Judging by the size of the traffic jam, he was going to be here for a while. "Not happening. Not today," he said aloud, his voice sounding hollow even to his own ears. It was times like these when he wished he could fly. How he'd do it without any mortals noticing him sailing through the air he had no idea, but he'd make it work, if it meant he could get to Krista that much faster. What was the use of having wings if they were just for show?

"Call Gunther," he activated the hands-free phone system and waited for his brother to answer.

"Magnuson."

"Gunth. I'm stuck in a clusterfuck of stopped cars on the damned highway!"

"Out on I-4? Ah, shit. There's an accident out there. With injuries. It's gonna be awhile."

"I don't have time, Gunther." Desperation made his voice crack.

"I know, man. We'll get her, brother."

"Not if I'm stuck on this fucking highway!"

"Okay, calm down. Are you in one of the outer lanes? Can you move your vehicle over to the breakdown lane?"

Gregor looked out his side mirrors, gauging the distance. "I can manage that."

"Do that and put your flashers on. I'll notify my guys of the situation, so they won't tag you. Then sit tight. I'm on my way."

His brother ended the call and Gregor did as Gunther instructed and waited.

It seemed like an eternity before his car appeared behind him. Gregor got out, hit lock on the key fob, and slid into the passenger seat of his brother's patrol car.

"Thanks for the lift."

"You betcha. Now tell me what you know so we can get your lady back."

With a sigh, Gregor pinched the bridge of his nose, squeezing his eyes shut. "That's just it, Gunth. I don't know anything. When I got up this morning she was," he paused, "gone. No sign of her."

"How'd you not hear her leave?"

"Uh, I was sleeping really well."

His brother gave him a look of disbelief. "Since when?"

Gregor wasn't one to kiss and tell, but his expression must've given him away.

Acknowledgement dawned on his brother's features. "You slept together. When did that happen?"

"Last night."

"Brother, you've done it now. Krista Wallingford must be one special woman if you broke your vow to never again sleep with a client." Gunther whistled.

"That's the reason she's in trouble."

"How'd you figure?"

"If we hadn't," he paused, searching for the right words, and came up with none, "been together last night, I wouldn't have slept so well. I would've remained alert instead of comfortably numb."

"It was that good, huh? So, totally worth it."

"This isn't funny. She could be in real trouble and I have no idea where to find her."

Gunther pulled the car into a designated space. "I'm not making light of the situation. I just never thought I'd see the day come where you would break. We'll track Thaddeus down and find out where he's taken her. Let's go in and get to work."

Gregor followed his brother into the station.

"You want coffee?" He stopped in front of a coffee maker with a full pot and poured himself a cup.

"No, thanks."

They continued to Gunther's office, and Gregor watched, surprised that no one around them paying them any attention. Gunther walked around his desk and took a seat, then grabbed a notepad from a desk drawer, and snagged a pen from the MBPD mug sitting on his desk.

"Let's talk about where we're at and what we know. When was the last time you saw Krista?"

"Seriously?"

"Ah, never mind. I guess we already established that she was with you all night. "His brother raised an eyebrow in question. "She was, right?"

"Yes!"

"What was the last interaction you had with Thaddeus?"

"The same time as you. At that club where he ghosted us."

"You haven't heard from him since then?"

Gregor shook his head. "Not personally. Some emails that

he sent, and that message from the other day, but he hasn't shown his face." He sighed. "I haven't caught his scent until this morning."

Gunther pushed back his chair and stood. "Well, Brother, let's go on a field trip. We should be able to track his scent from your suite. It'll give us a place to start."

It was worth a shot. Gregor just hoped they weren't too late. *Hold on, Krista. I'm coming for you, love.*

CHAPTER FOURTEEN

Krista's skull was pounding as her eyes fluttered open. She rubbed the back of her head and winced at the sore spot where her head had met the wall. It was bleeding. The room spun as she sat up in the same room and bed she was in earlier.

The walls blurred. She was pretty sure she had a concussion. Her captor really cares about her, huh? She could've gone to sleep never to wake back up and then he'd have been guilty of murder. Or maybe he didn't care and that was his end game anyway.

She knew Gregor would come to her rescue. Not that she was some damsel in distress, but right now she held little hope of getting herself out of this situation alone. He had to be looking for her.

His brother was a cop. Gunther should be able to offer some assistance. He had to. She couldn't stay here.

Thank God he hadn't raped her. But she really didn't know what he wanted. His talk about, what did he call it? The otherworld? What the hell was that.

His face. She remembered his face. The memory was

fuzzy, but she saw him change his face. Now who was the one with the crazy issue? That couldn't have really happened. It was impossible.

But why was he so adamant about making her believe that the supernatural was real? It was just all so weird.

The door opened with a creak and her captor entered, kicking the door closed with a booted foot, holding a bottle of water in his hand.

"I noticed you wouldn't drink from a glass, so I brought you this." He held the bottle out for her to take. "Smart thinking. One never knows what might have been slipped into it. Not that I would dare, but others might."

Krista snorted, "Really? Others might? Not you? You drugged me to get me here?" She took the bottle and examined the seam on the cap to make sure the seal hadn't been broken.

"That was different."

"Not really. Not at all, actually. It's the same exact thing." She twisted the cap off and took a long pull of the water. It was warm, but she was so thirsty, it didn't matter.

The way his eyes bored into her, head cocked to the left side, creeped her out. His leer sent shivers down her spine.

"Are you going to let me out of this room?"

He shrugged. "Depends."

"On what?"

"Are you going to run?"

She wanted to scream at the top of her lungs, *of course she was going to run!* She had to get out of here, but she knew telling him the truth would get her nowhere, so she lied through her teeth. "No."

He smiled, showing yellow, crooked teeth. "Good. I wouldn't want to hurt you and if you run, that's what I'll do." He clapped his hands together, as if washing away the subject of inflicting bodily harm on her and asked, "Are you hungry?"

She wasn't. Food was the last thing on her mind, but she would need the energy to keep her mind clear so she could keep an eye out for any small chance of escape.

"Ah, I see you're worried about me drugging the food. Not to worry. You're not going anywhere."

The matter-of-fact way he stated that did nothing to put her at ease. She was fairly certain he was telling the truth about not putting anything in her food. If eating whatever he had was a way to get out of this room and into another part of the house or whatever it was he was holding her in, then she'd say she was starving.

"Follow me. And don't do anything stupid," he threw over his shoulder as he walked toward the door. "We can finish our conversation over dinner."

She stood and wobbled on her feet. Using the mattress for balance, she waited a few long moments before taking a step. Fairly certain that her legs weren't going to give out, she met him in the hallway where he was waiting for her to join him.

He walked slowly, allowing her to keep up, talking the whole time. He waved his hand to either side, "all of these doors are locked. Just rooms that aren't used."

She looked around. There was nothing distinctive marks anywhere to clue her in on where she was. The hall was plain, the walls painted slate gray with navy blue doors. It was dark and depressing and didn't lend Krista any comfort.

They took a left at the end of the hall and walked into an outdated kitchen that had seen its glory days in the seventies. Formica covered countertops were bare except for a coffee maker and a drying rack for dishes.

A small table for two, laminated in the same design as the counters was bumped up against the wall to allow room to maneuver around it. A small olive-green fridge hummed along loudly, sounding like it could die at any minute.

He pointed to one of the chairs, "take a seat."

She pulled out one of the chairs, made from that weird plastic cushion material so popular in decades past. The kind your skin stuck to when it was hot out and you were wearing shorts. At least she had leggings on. She didn't even want to think about the number of other people's skin that had touched the same seat.

A shudder rippled through her.

"Do you have a chill?" I can turn down the A/C."

Lord no! "No, I'm fine. Thank you." She thought about how to get him talking again. It was the only way to figure out how to get the hell out of here. "If you don't mind me asking, what's your name? I mean, if we're going to be spending all this time together, I should at least know your name." Plus, if she found out she could somehow pass the information along to Gregor.

He looked up from the sandwich he was making, as if weighing whether or not he'd tell her, before nodding in agreement. "Thaddeus."

An odd name that she'd never heard before, kind of like Gregor and his brother. But they weren't originally from the states and the hint of an accent she heard whenever they spoke was Scottish. She couldn't remember how long Gregor had said he'd lived here. And until he told her where he was from, she'd had no idea. And Gregor. Not Greg. Not Gregory. But Gregor. It was just an odd name. Gunther, too.

"It's an old family name, you could say. It's been in our family for eons."

Again, a weird word choice. *Eons.*

THADDEUS FEARED that he revealed too much. Krista seemed to be contemplating what he said about his name a bit too long.

He may have whacked her head good and stunned her for a bit, but her senses were definitely sharpening. At first, he'd thought he'd given her a concussion, but decided it was just a good old crack.

It didn't seem to do any lasting damage. She had some blood from the cut on the back of her head, but she'd be fine.

He hoped she liked bologna sandwiches. It was all he could snag at the corner grocery just down the street. He probably should've picked up some potato chips. Isn't that what Americans liked to eat with their sandwiches? Or pickles. Alas, he hadn't thought of either of those so she'd have to deal with what he was giving her.

On white bread, no less. He wasn't going to waste his time on this side eating wheat bread. Where was the enjoyment in that? Humans nowadays with their chia seed breads or whatever they put in the damn loaf to make it less like bread and more like a granola. Food is meant to be savored.

He placed a paper plate on the table and sat across from Krista. Paper plates. Another convenience in modern times that he wished he'd had all along. Makes cleanup a jiffy!

"Thank you." She said, nervously eyeing the sandwich.

"It's bologna and cheese. No drugs. Do you want a pop?"

"No, thanks." She tentatively took a bite. He watched her chew. Enjoyed the up and down motion of her jaw.

"You're going to make a lovely bride."

She choked and coughed on the bite of sandwich that was in her mouth. "Excuse me?"

"When we get married. You're going to be beautiful."

She dropped the sandwich on the plate and pushed the chair from the table in a swift motion. Too swift, because she swayed on her feet, before catching herself and regaining her balance. Her eyes darted around the kitchen, probably searching for something she could use as a weapon, but there was nothing.

He'd made sure of that. It's why her sandwich didn't have any condiments. He didn't want to have to use a knife to spread it.

"Really, Krista. Sit back down and eat your dinner. You haven't had anything to eat for hours. You need sustenance."

"You're crazy."

"I know you think that now but imagine everything I can show you. The world that's out there." He stood, then walked up to her and touched his finger gently to the tip of her nose. "Right under your pretty little nose and you don't even see it." He spun. "Open your mind to the possibilities. It's all so amazing."

"You really are crazy. There's no other reason. You can't possibly believe what you are saying."

"My dear, I don't need to believe it. I live it every day." And with that, to prove his point, he changed into his own form, his face changing in front of her.

His heart skipped a beat at the way her eyes widened in fear. It wasn't his intention to frighten her, but he'd be denying the truth if he said it didn't give him a small thrill.

"See. The world in front of you as you know it is so much more than you can see." He guided her back to her chair. "Sit back down. Finish eating."

He went to the refrigerator and grabbed a can of soda. Even though she'd denied it earlier, he was thinking she'd want something to drink and he didn't have any liquor to offer her, so soda would have to do.

"Here."

Her beautiful face was pale. Not like her natural color of ivory, more like all the blood had drained out of her face.

"There's no reason for you to be frightened. We've always

walked among you." He rolled his eyes. "We're sworn to secrecy. Forbidden to show ourselves to the mortals. But, you. You're different. I knew the first time I saw you that you would be the one I would tell that it's not only humans walking this earth."

Her eyes widened even more. He feared they may pop out of their sockets if she didn't pull herself together.

"What are you?" She asked quietly.

"I believe in your mythical books you call me a skin walker." He threw his hands up in the air. "Surprise! We're real!"

She shook her head. "That's not possible."

"But it is, my darling." He covered her hand with his, but she quickly withdrew it as if scorched by his touch. "We were here before you humans were even a thought."

THE BROTHERS TRACKED THADDEUS' scent into the parking lot of the hotel. There, the smell of the skin walker mixed with diesel all but disappeared.

"Not as many diesel vehicles on the road. That might help us."

"Does Krista have her phone? Or did you find it in the suite?"

"It's definitely not in the suite."

Gunther smiled. "That's our in. Let's head back to the station." He turned and headed back to the patrol car.

Gregor followed on his brother's heels. "What are you talking about?"

"We can track her phone."

"I'm sure her phone's been turned off by now." Thaddeus wasn't all that familiar with this world, but Gregor was pretty sure he knew about cell tracking.

"Maybe. But we can at least get the tracking info. Chances

are he was in too much of a hurry to turn off her phone when he grabbed her."

"I'm not following."

"If he didn't, then we can follow the trail. The phone is going to ping off nearby cell towers as it passes. We find the last place the phone pinged off of, and we set up a radius to search. That's our starting point."

"I guess."

"Do you have a better idea? We've found a lot of people using cell tracking. Of course, if you know her cloud details, we can log in and track her via GPS."

"Why would I have that?"

"I don't know. Maybe since you two were becoming close she decided to share. How do you think all these celebs have their personal photos published all the time? They can't keep that info to themselves."

Back at the station, Gregor hovered over the officer that was working his cyber magic and beginning to come up with a route that took Krista away from the coast of Moon Bay and brought her further inland.

If Gregor ever wanted to change up his profession, cyber forensics could be interesting. The guy looked over his shoulder. "Man, you gotta give me some space."

"Sorry," he muttered and stepped back to pace the floor. He was too anxious waiting for a lead. Something, anything that would lead him to Krista.

Memories of Katherine crept into his mind. The fear he felt when he'd discovered her missing was nothing compared to what he was feeling now. When he'd found her lifeless body, his world crashed. He'd failed the one person he was supposed to protect. That was when he'd vowed to never get physically or emotionally involved with a client ever again.

Then he saw Krista and all barriers crumbled. His vows

broken. And to what end? He prayed silently to the Gods above. She had to be okay.

Minutes passed like hours until finally they had some answers. The officer who told him to leave earlier approached and held out a piece of paper. "We've narrowed it down to a small radius. Her phone isn't off, so it's still pinging off a tower on the edge of the city." He looked grim.

"That's great. So, what's the issue?"

The guy shrugged. "It's not the best area. A lot of warehouses. It's gonna be a bitch trying to get in there unnoticed."

Gunther rounded the corner and joined them. "It won't be an issue. Thanks for working your magic, Sykes." He took the address and motioned for Gregor to follow him.

"You know the area?" Gregor asked, walking shoulder to shoulder with his brother, their hulking figures filling the hallway.

"Yeah. There's not a lot of foot traffic, which works in our favor, but also against us."

"How so?"

"With no normal foot traffic, anyone showing up in that area is going to draw suspicion. If Thaddeus has people watching we'll be had pretty quickly."

"I doubt he's been able to muster a team. I'm pretty sure he came here for one reason. To get his filthy hands on Krista." Gregor's stomach lurched at the thought of Krista being stuck somewhere with Thaddeus. If he hurt her in any way. Gregor didn't care if it was as little as a split end, he was going to kill the bastard.

"Easy, brother."

Gregor looked at Gunther, his vision going cloudy around the edges. He swore and willed himself to calm down. His anger had gotten the best of him and he was starting to shift to his gargoyle form. Not something that he could do here.

"We'll find them both."

"Thaddeus is going to pay. I'll make sure of it."

"I have no doubt. Does the skin walker know what you drive?"

"I'm assuming so. There's no way to know when and where he was watching Krista, but I'm sure he started not long after we got here. But my truck's stuck on the highway."

"Let's head to my house and grab my car. Can't show up in the marked SUV, that will draw too much attention. And we can pick up Bones while we're there."

"Bones?"

"My dog. He loves adventure."

"Didn't picture you as the dog type." Gregor tilted his head to the side. "More of a cat person. The real fluffy kind."

"Fuck you, man."

Gregor let out a small laugh. The first he'd had in a while.

CHAPTER FIFTEEN

G unther's house wasn't what Gregor had expected. The Mediterranean modern-style ranch was a far cry from the family home they grew up in.

Inside, the three-bedroom house was decorated straight from the bachelor's pad magazine if there ever was one. Large, black leather couches lined two walls of the living room, flanking a huge television screen hanging from the wall. A casino table served as a coffee table between the two sofa's and a massive recliner was set off catty corner.

"Nice place."

Gunth shot him a look letting Gregor know he didn't believe him. That he knew sarcasm when he heard it.

"What?" Gregor held his hands up in defense. "I'm serious. I mean, if you have the guys over all the time, it's the perfect place for you all to hang out."

"Funny."

"Well, you don't bring women here, do you?"

"Why wouldn't I? You may be surprised to find out that I'm no saint. Celibacy is not in my vocab."

"Yeah, okay, killer. Calm down. I'm not the one trying to get in your pants."

Gunther shook his head. "You're such an ass. There's a reason we went years without talking to each other." He walked over to the back door and opened it up and a hundred pounds of black and brown fur came barreling through, jumping on Gunther, and licking his face to welcome him home.

Gregor stood off to the side, anxious for them to get back on the road. Any minute added to their time was a minute that could mean life or death for Krista.

His brother greeted Bones with a rub to his head before the dog noticed someone else was in the house.

The Rottweiler loped over to Gregor, sniffing, but not growling.

"Here, boy!" Gregor said and squatted down. The dog lost all his inhibitions and came at Gregor full force, knocking them both to the ground before licking his face in greeting.

"He seems to like you," Gunther stated. "Makes one of us."

"You're hilarious. We gotta get going. We need to get to Krista."

"Gotcha." Gunther grabbed a leash off a hook by the front door and called the dog. "Bones, come."

With one last lick and muzzle nudge, Bones left Gregor on the floor and joined Gunther. He snapped the leash to his spiked collar and glanced at his brother. "You gonna lay on the floor all night or are you going to help me get your woman back?" he tossed over his shoulder as he headed out the door and into the driveway.

Gregor hopped up to his feet and brushed his ass off. Seemed Gunther found his sense of humor in his old age, and he wasn't sure if he liked it.

With Bones in the back seat, gnawing on a pig's ear, they headed out to the warehouse district. If Krista was truly there, Gregor wouldn't believe their luck. To think that Thaddeus hadn't turned off her phone was amazing. Maybe the skin walker didn't understand technology. Or maybe he was just that stupid. But if it worked, he wouldn't complain. He could practically kiss the guy for his ignorance.

After he kicked his ass for taking Krista in the first place. His hands clenched into fists at his side, he wasn't big on violence, but the thought of pounding his fists into the soft flesh of Thaddeus's face gave him more thrills than he'd like to admit.

That fucker was going to pay. He'll wish he'd stayed in the Otherworld by the time Gregor was done with him and handed him over to the Superior Council, begging them to take him back.

WAS GREGOR LOOKING FOR HER? Did he even notice she was gone? She'd like to think they shared some kind of connection last night when their bodies had come together in a passion she hadn't experienced with another person...ever.

The whole experience was something new. Feelings had been awakened that she just couldn't imagine having with someone else. And she'd been with a lot of guys. Not something she was necessarily proud of, but it was the truth.

She'd always been searching for that special someone. The person that would take her away and make her forget everything that was wrong in her world.

Gregor Magnuson was that person. Krista didn't worry about anything when she was with him. She knew he'd take care of her and keep her safe.

She laughed. Finding it oddly ironic that the person she felt most safe with was also the person that hadn't protected her as he was hired to do and now she found herself cooped up with a madman that could somehow change his face.

She still had no idea how he managed to do that. Was it magic? An illusion? Or some kind of mind trick? She didn't know and it freaked her out.

But not as much as the talk about marrying him. The guy was truly fucking insane. Like she would ever marry him. Not willingly, anyway. She just prayed Gregor would find her before she was forced to go through Thaddeus' mad plan.

The door burst open, and the nutcase came barreling in. "My darling, look what I've brought you." He set a white rectangular box on the bed beside her and stepped back. "Well, open it," he urged when she didn't move.

A million bucks she could guess what was in the damn box and she didn't want that piece of information confirmed, so she just sat there. Maybe if she ignored him, he'd go away.

"Fine, you're shy. I understand." He moved forward and grasped the corners of the cover. "Let me assist you." He tugged and pulled the top off the box. She'd guessed right Inside was a wedding dress. Thaddeus smiled at her. She wished he wouldn't. The gesture did nothing to transform his face into something sincere. It just made him look even more ghoulish than he already did. How did she not notice that when he was on the movie set?

How did none of them notice? Even Gregor who was always so observant about everything. Most of the time, annoyingly too observant. Yet, he hadn't figured it out either.

"Well, what do you think, my love?" He asked, holding up the white lace atrocity he'd pulled from the box. "It matches your skin tone perfectly," he held the material close to her for comparison. "There's even a matching veil in here," he dug around in the box and came away with a band of pink, artificial flowers and a mid-length gossamer veil.

Pink flowers? He knew she had red hair, right? They

would clash something awful. But not as awful as actually wearing them to marry this maniac.

Krista sat quietly. She didn't want to encourage him and make him think that she was on board with this idea. But she didn't want to piss him off either, and make him to do something drastic either. Her head still pounded from the beating she'd received earlier.

"I think you'll be happy in my world. With me. Us. We'll make a wonderful couple."

"I need to use the restroom." She didn't, but she didn't want to be in his space any longer.

"Of course. Let me draw you a bath."

The thought of bathing with him near was horrifying. "No, no. I'll take one later. Right now, I just..." she paused, "I had a lot to drink, so..."

Understanding finally dawned in his eyes and he nodded. "Yes, of course. I'll give you some privacy. Let me go unlock it for you." He left and returned a few minutes later. "Don't get any funny ideas. You know I'll just find you if you do and as much as I disliked hurting you last time, I won't hesitate to do it again." His look sent tremors of terror down Krista's spine. His eyes were so dead. Cold. Cruel.

She nodded. "I understand."

He smiled. "Good. Follow me."

He led her down the hall to a door that was already opened. Once she was inside, he slammed it shut and she heard the lock slip in place. Her heart sank.

Was she really surprised? Not after her last escape attempt. She studied the room. It was small and utilitarian. It lacked the comfort of a household bathroom, giving her the impression that this was a business bathroom. There was no linen closet. Just a white toilet, a sink with no vanity and a small tub and shower combo. The shower curtain was a clear plastic liner.

However, there was a window. It was small and square, but it did open. Quietly, she stepped into the tub and tested it. It was locked. Not giving up, she flipped the latch and pushed up.

It didn't budge. She looked closer and found that the window was sealed shut with caulking all around. Maybe she could break it and alert whoever was outside. If there even was anyone outside. She couldn't see anyone out there, the privacy glass only letting her know it was dark out. But Thaddeus would hear the glass break and she'd be screwed. There had to be another way, she just had to find it. And fast.

There was a towel by the sink, and if she could wrap it around her arm to muffle the sound. And if she could muster enough strength to break the glass, she could climb out. But, was there enough space? It would be tight. Nothing in the small room could be used to barricade the door, so she needed to move fast.

Soon, Thaddeus would come checking in on her, wondering what was taking her so long. Unless she could convince him that she wanted to take a bath now. The running water would muffle the sound of the glass breaking too. It might give her a better chance to get away.

She flushed the toilet and washed her hands, and not surprisingly, the door unlocked and her captor poked his head in.

"I was thinking, I could really use a bath now. I think I'm ready."

His whole face lit up. "I knew it! I knew you'd see the light."

Inwardly, Krista cringed at the thought, but she plastered a smile on her face. "It's a lot to take in, but I get it."

"This is going to be wonderful. Hold tight. I'll grab you some towels and supplies. "He closed the door and the lock sounded again. This could most definitely work in her favor.

THE WAREHOUSE DISTRICT in Moon Bay consisted of two streets on the outer edge of the city. The layout of the concrete buildings reminded Gregor more of an industrial park than warehouses, but who was he to tell them they were naming things incorrectly.

Streetlights lined both roads and lit the area up like the fourth of July. Gunther parked and they exited the vehicle, Bones hopping out and trotting along beside them.

Gregor looked up, studying the buildings and sniffed the air. Nothing stood out.

"What's our game plan?" Gunther asked. "Do you have something in mind?"

"We need to be able to maneuver around and get a dial on these buildings before we decide on a plan of action. But we need to do it quick, though. I want to get to Krista as soon as possible."

"Heard. Let's split up," Gunther said, "Walk the perimeter and then meet back here."

"Unless you find something." Gregor said. "Then you better call me right away."

Gunther shook his head and reached into his pocket and drew out the slip of material Gregor had given him earlier. One of Krista's silk headbands. He held it out for Bones to sniff. "I'm hoping he can hone in on Krista even better than we can."

"We'll see." Gregor said, praying he was right.

"I'll take the left. You take the right and we'll meet back here in ten. Sound good?"

Gregor gave a curt nod and headed toward the nearest building. The windows were all dark. Nothing going on in that one. And the next building was the same. The third, a brick building, had lights on inside.

He stopped and put his hands on the brick, listening. He didn't hear any movement inside and he didn't catch Krista's scent.

He continued his search, the soles of his boots thudding along the pavement. But, there was no sign of her.

And then he heard it. It was faint. The slightest crack of glass. He grabbed his phone and dialed Gunther. "Meet me at," he searched the facade of the building for a number, "1580. I think I got something."

"On my way."

This building was concrete, painted dark gray, with designs etched into the masonry work. There were no lights illuminating the windows of the upper floors but down toward the street level, a few rooms were lit.

His brother silently joined him, Bones on his heels, tongue lolling.

"I heard glass break somewhere in this area."

They continued to examine the area, looking closely at the lower windows.

Thunk!

The brothers looked up simultaneously to see a figure pushing against one of the windows.

"Krista!"

A face pressed to the small fissure. "Gregor? Oh, my God. Gregor! Is that you?" Her panic-laced voice came out in a hushed whisper.

"It's me, Baby. Hold on. We're gonna get you out." He eyed the height of the window. It was out of his reach. There was no way he could break through it the rest of the way from his position.

Gunther seemed to know what he was thinking. "I can do it." After a quick look around, his brother shifted into his gargoyle form and took flight, hovering just outside the window. "Krista, step back from the window."

"Hurry! He's going to come in any minute!"

As his brother started picking away at the glass, careful to not spray Krista with the shards, Gregor could hear the fear in her voice.

He needed to get inside and confront Thaddeus. He looped around to the front and slipped into the door, which to his surprise was unlocked. Not what he was expecting. He ascended the staircase, careful to keep as quiet as possible, all the while listening for any noises that would help him figure out where exactly they were in the building.

The halls were dark, but Gregor had no problem seeing. His sight was better at night than during the day. He shifted into his gargoyle form and stalked down the hall.

Around the next corner, the hallway opened into a large room. Gregor glanced around. Someone had been in here recently. Plates and bottles were on the table, and fluorescent lights hummed overhead. He could hear running water.

He started toward the sound and then stopped, straining his ears. Was that humming?

Was the motherfucker actually humming along as if nothing out of the ordinary was happening?

He crept closer to the sound, careful not to make any noise to alert the skin walker that he was here. When the walker came into view, Gregor took a step back.

The creature was in his natural form. An unpleasant sight for anyone that laid eyes upon him. Is that the face he'd shown Krista? Gods. She must be terrified.

Thaddeus turned and the song on his lips died as he noticed Gregor, the material he'd held in his hands floated to the floor. Gregor paid the item no attention as he descended upon the walker, grabbing him by his throat and holding him up against the wall.

"Where is she?" He growled, his teeth bared.

The walker's fingers scratched at Gregor's huge fist, trying to get him to loosen his grip.

"I swear to the Gods, Thaddeus, if you hurt as much as one hair on Krista's beautiful head, I'm going to fucking kill you. Slowly. Painfully."

"You can't. You need to return me to the Council, Guardian." He spat. "I know the rules."

Gregor slammed him into the wall again. "I don't care about the rules when it comes to Krista."

Thaddeus stuttered. "She agreed to marry me. Did you get that far with her? She believes in us. I finally made her see."

Gregor rammed his fist into the soft flesh of the skin walker's face, feeling bones crush from the impact. As much as Gregor wanted to continue to beat Thaddeus's face into a bloody pulp, his first priority was Krista. He knew she was safe in his brother's hands, but he needed to see for himself. He reached for the cuffs he'd grabbed earlier and slapped them around the skin walker's wrists, securing them around a metal drainage pipe.

He turned and ran down the hall, toward the sound of running water. "Krista!"

"Gregor!" She yelled, the sweet sound of her voice urging him forward. "I'm here! The door is locked from the outside. I can't open it."

"Stand back!" He hefted his shoulder against the door and the frame splintered and gave. Relief washed over him as he laid eyes on Krista. She was safe. But bruised. He took in the purple bump on the side of her face and saw red.

Moving forward to wrap her in his arms, he was totally taken aback by her scream of pure terror, before she crumpled to the floor in an unconscious heap.

And that's when he'd realized he was still in his gargoyle form.

Fuck.

CHAPTER SIXTEEN

Krista's eyes fluttered open. Gregor stopped touching her all over making sure she was alright. "Did he hurt you?"

She shook her head and relief flooded through his adrenaline pumped veins.

"Thank the Gods." He crushed her to him and nearly melted when she wrapped her arms around his waist. He looked into her eyes, and saw the fire burning in their brown depths. Her lips parted slightly, and that was the only sign he needed. He dropped his head and captured her mouth in a kiss and almost died when she responded just as feverishly.

"Umm, I hate to interrupt this love fest," Gunther interjected, "but, we really need to get out of here before we draw attention to ourselves."

Sadly, Gregor pulled away from Krista, but loved the look of passion glowing in her eyes.

"Um, I could've sworn you had, um... I'm sorry, I think I'm losing my mind. It must be the drugs. I'm pretty sure that guy slipped something into my food."

Gregor exchanged a look with his brother, and Gunther

shrugged. "You might as well tell her. She's going to find out eventually."

"Find out what?"

"What exactly did Thaddeus say to you?"

"That guy, and I use the term very loosely, is bat shit crazy. He talked about making me immortal. And about things I've only read about. At times he was very convincing. But those things are impossible. Creatures living in another world. In our world. That's impossible. Right?"

He wrestled with how to break the truth to her. Would she run? Think he was fucking with her? Or that he was batshit crazy, too?

"Maybe we'll just take things slow for now."

"What things? Just tell me."

"How about I just show you?"

Krista looked at him weird. "You guys are freaking me out. More than I've already been freaked out by acid trip over there." She pointed to Thaddeus, who was slumped on the floor, watching Gregor warily.

"You should sit." After he settled her safely in the one of the chairs, he took a few steps back, drew in a deep breath and shifted into gargoyle form.

Krista's eyes widened and her mouth formed an 'O', right before she fainted.

KRISTA WOKE up in her hotel room to the smell of coffee and bacon. Last night she'd had the weirdest dream, and even now she was still feeling a little out of it, so she rolled out of bed and padded into the bathroom and saw that she wasn't in her pajamas, but the skirt and blouse from her dream. That was weird. She never slept in her clothes. They cost way too much to do that. Then after a quick glance in the mirror she realized her face was smudged with makeup, a huge bruise covered her whole cheek. What the hell was going on? What happened? She always washed her face before she went to bed. She had a strict routine she kept to religiously. She was determined to age naturally and gracefully.

Something was definitely off. Maybe a nice hot shower would clear the cobwebs out of her mind. She stripped and started the shower. As she turned back to the mirror, she noticed dark colored bruises on her arms. She touched them tenderly, wincing at the pain. Visions of wings and stone flooded her memory.

Leaving the water running, she ran into her room and rummaged around for her pajamas before stalking into the kitchen.

Gregor, dressed in jeans and a tight tee shirt was bent over a frying pan, cooking bacon. He turned when he heard her, the smile on his full lips dying when he took note of her expression.

"You! You're...you're...who the hell are you?" She looked around the kitchen and grabbed the closest thing she could find...the mug of steaming hot coffee he'd just poured for her. "What are you?"

He put his hands up, still holding onto a spatula. "Krista. Sit. I'm not going to hurt you. I promise."

He sounded sincere. But could she trust him?

Putting the spatula down, he turned off the stove and backed away to the far side of the kitchen. Making sure to keep his distance.

"I swear I'd never hurt you. I was hired to protect you."

"From a fucking nightmare."

"True. But I couldn't just tell you that. We have rules."

"Really? Like shocking the hell out of humans?"

"No. We don't really make ourselves known."

"What are you? I mean, I see this you, but what are you

really?"

"I'm human, just like you."

She shook her head. "No, not like me. I can't transform into a fucking monster." She hated the way her voice rose, becoming trill even to her own ears. "I want the truth. What are you?"

He sighed, hanging his head. "My mother was a human. My father, on the other hand, is a gargoyle. My brother, like me, is a hybrid."

"He can fly? He was hovering outside the bathroom window last night."

"Yeah, but I can't."

"Can't what?"

"I've got wings, but they're useless. I can't fly."

"I thought you turned to stone during the day? Isn't that how it works? I used to watch this show and as soon as the sun came up, they turned to stone. But you. You're not."

Gregor shook his head. "That's one of my hybrid characteristics. I don't have the sunlight curse. Same with all my siblings. None of us turn to stone during the day. We can thank our mum for that. Now, our dad on the other hand." His voice trailed off.

"What about your dad?" She asked, curious to know more. To try to fathom what he was telling her.

"Our dad is full gargoyle. So, he has the sunlight curse. During the day, he's stone and goes deep down into the family estate to be safe from anyone he may encounter while he's vulnerable."

She pressed her hand to her forehead. "I can't believe this is happening." Amazement filled her, but she was still wary.

"Krista," he approached her slowly. Cautiously. "I swear I won't hurt you."

She let him come closer. So close now, they were practically touching.

"And Thaddeus. He's a gargoyle, too?"

"Oh, Gods, no! He's a skin walker."

She had no idea what that was.

"He has the ability to take on the look of anyone or anything he comes in contact with."

"That explains a lot. Are there others?"

"Other skin walkers?"

"No. Yes, but, other, I don't know what you call them. Beings?"

"Supernaturals? Yes. Pretty much everything you've ever heard about is real."

"This is crazy. I have so many questions. I just..I can't. I don't know what to think." Looking into his eyes, he looked so sincere.

"I know. And I'll answer them all. I swear. But for now, can you trust me?"

She gazed into his pleading eyes. As much as her mind screamed no, yelled at her that she was insane, her heart said otherwise. She knew she was safe with him.

She nodded.

He opened his arms and she fell into them, knowing that this was where she was supposed to be.

"We can talk about all this later. Right now, I have some business I need to tend to."

"What?"

"I need to deliver Thaddeus to the Council. It's part of our world. I promise I'll explain it all to you, but for now, I need to take him back to where he belongs. Gunther's going to stay with you while I take care of that, okay?"

Krista drew in a deep, shaky breath. Still a bit unsure if she was safe or if she should be concerned. Never mind her sanity. She was pretty sure she'd lost that. "Okay."

A knock sounded at the door and Gregor let Gunther into their suite. Krista studied them both. Their hulking frames filling the large space and making it seem small. "And there are more of you?"

Gunther lifted a brow in question.

Gregor cleared his throat? "Gargoyle hybrids?"

She couldn't believe she was saying yes to that but nodded her head.

"We come from a pretty big family, but outside of the Magnuson's, I don't think so. At least we haven't run across any yet." He gave her a wink, then bent and kissed her forehead. "And I'll be more than happy to tell you more about my pain in the ass family. But I have to take care of this first. I'll be back as soon as I can."

As soon as the door shut behind Gregor, Krista felt alone, even with Gunther right beside her. It was a strange feeling. She missed him already.

GREGOR PUSHED Thaddeus to his knees in front of The Council, the bruises from the beating he'd given the skin walker still visible against his pale skin.

Gregor took pride in those bruises.

"Splendid work, Magnuson. You'll be paid well for your services. As for you, Thaddeus, you know the punishment for breaking your retirement contract. Freedom is no longer yours." The Vampire Superior stated.

Thaddeus glared at Gregor but stayed silent.

With a nod from The Council, two armed guards stepped forward and cuffed Thaddeus before hauling him away.

"What's his sentence?" Gregor asked.

"Not your concern. The Council thanks you again for your service. Until next time, Magnuson. Dismissed."

Fuck them and their secretive ways. He had to get back to Krista.

Knowing he would get no further information, he bowed and turned to leave the hall.

"Magnuson!"

Gregor turned, facing The Council once again.

"Come forward." This time it was the Fairy Superior giving orders, her small size deceiving to the power she held.

Gregor walked back to The Superiors and paused in front of them, feet planted.

"It has been brought to our attention that you have broken the creed of The Dark Moor Guardians by alerting humans to your presence."

He didn't say a word. They hadn't asked him a question.

"Speak!" The Fairy Superior yelled, her voice echoing off the palace's walls.

"It is true. I had no choice but to use my gargoyle form while I was saving the human from Thaddeus." He hated to refer to Krista as 'the human', but that's all The Council would see her as.

The Council murmured amongst themselves, before nodding in agreement over whatever they were discussing.

"As punishment, you will not be paid for this assignment. Now, leave! We will be in contact."

He didn't give a shit about the money. That was the most they could do. They couldn't remove him as a Guardian. He was the best they had out there.

Walking quickly, he exited the hall, not wanting to spend any more time in there than needed.

Krista was waiting for him in Moon Bay. And he couldn't wait to get back to her.

They had a lot to talk about if they were going to make this work.

And for the first time in his long life, he knew he'd found *the one*.

He just had to convince her of the same.

CHAPTER SEVENTEEN

Gregor unlocked the door to the suite and strode past his brother who was rinsing a glass in the sink.

"Hey, how'd it go with The Council?"

"Good. Where's Krista?" He paused in the living room, noticing she wasn't there.

"In the shower." Gunther set the glass on the sideboard to dry. "Did they say anything?"

"Nothing more than usual."

Gunther looked disappointed. Gregor knew his brother longed to be a Guardian. He'd played a big part in saving Krista. He vowed to mention that to The Council. Maybe if he put in a good word, he might get his chance.

"Thanks, man. I wouldn't have been able to get Krista back safely without your help." He smiled sheepishly. "Even Guardians need help sometimes."

His brother nodded, bobbing his head up and down. "Yeah, anytime. We good?" He wiped his hands on a bleached white towel before folding it in half and hanging it on the rack. "I gotta get back."

"Gunth?" His brother paused on his way to the door. "I'm glad we, uh," he swallowed nervously. "We reconnected."

Pale eyes crinkling, Gunther's face split into a wide smile. "Me too, bro. See you around?"

"That's a promise." And Gregor meant it this time. He watched his brother leave and then latched the door, before heading into Krista's bathroom, stripping his clothes along the way.

Steam fogged the mirror and rolled off the walls, rising in curls toward the fan in the middle of the room. Music blared from the portable speaker she'd set on the bathroom vanity, masking his entry.

"You're so beautiful."

Krista turned with a yelp. "Jesus! Gregor! You need to stop sneaking up on me. You scared me!"

"Sorry." He opened the glass door of the shower and slipped inside, wrapping his arms around her and nuzzling her neck.

"I swear, I'm going to give you a necklace with a bell on it so you can't do that anymore." She lifted her arm and threaded her fingers through his short hair, rubbing his scalp. "Are you all set with..."

He watched her face as she searched for the words.

"Your boss? Manager?" She shrugged. "I don't even know what to call them."

Chuckling, he kissed her collarbone. She moaned and the vibration against his chest went straight to his dick. "It's all good. The Council was happy to have Thaddeus back." He nipped at her ear lobe.

She turned in his arms and pierced him with her chocolate brown eyes. "Did you get in trouble? About me?" Was that worry creasing her brow?

He planted a soft kiss on her forehead. "Don't worry about that. I'm good."

"You didn't answer my question," she stepped back. "Are you on bad terms with your council? I don't want to be the cause of you losing your job."

Gregor barked out a laugh and grasped her hand, pulling her closer, before planting a kiss in her wet palm. "Never going to happen. They need me too much." He worked his way up her arm, until her front was pressed against his, her body, heated from the water, molding to his. "We're good. I assure you. We can talk about it later." He flipped her around, so her back was against his front, his hand sliding down her stomach, lower, lower over the slick skin, until his fingers feathered over her wet folds.

Her breath hitched and a moan escaped her lips when he pushed a finger through her slick heat, and then another, drawing in and out until her breath came in short gasps.

Goosepimples raised her flesh under his hands even though the temp of the water was hot enough to keep her warm.

His hard length settled against her buttocks as his hands found her breasts. His fingers kneading her soft flesh before tweaking her nipples.

"Gregor!" His name echoed off the tile walls and he smiled, suckling at her neck for a moment longer.

When they were both gasping for breath, he lifted her onto his length and with a tilt of his hips, he entered her. Her tight sheath drawing him in until he was buried deep. Bracing her arms on the tile wall, she rode him, her long legs behind her, wrapped around him. His hands on her hips helping her movements.

"Mine." Gregor growled possessively, lifting her hips to quicken the pace, his breath coming in short grunts.

"Always." Krista answered, her voice breathy. "I'm so close."

In one swift move, Gregor pulled her body back to his

and for the briefest of seconds, broke their contact so he could turn her around, before lifting her again and sinking her on his cock. "I want to look at you when you come." He panted. "When we come together."

He drove into her warmth. Thrust after thrust.

Captured her mouth in his. His tongue plunging in rhythm with his cock.

"Gregor!" His name beautiful music to his ears. He could feel her body tightening around him. Her hands clawed and her nails scratched at his back. He reveled in the thought that she was marking him.

Hers.

Yeah, baby.

Wild with passion, he pistoned his hips, unable to slow his thrusts until his balls drew up and with a final push, his climax erupted with a holler of "Krista!" falling from his lips.

"WHAT ARE WE DOING?" They lay in her bed, blissfully sated, her head resting on Gregor's broad chest, a finger lazily drawing circles around a pale pink nipple, drawing it to a taut peak.

His big hand drew her head closer and he dropped a kiss on her hairline. "I think it was pretty obvious." She could hear the smile in his voice.

Lifting up on her elbows, she looked him in the eye. "Not that. Us. Is this really happening?"

Silver-blue eyes, the color swirling in that way that was uniquely Gregor, searched her face. "Do you want it to happen?"

She did. This...thing that they had going on. It felt real. So different from anything she'd ever experienced before.

"I do." She sighed. "But..." her voice trailed off.

Gregor sat up and leaned against the headboard, taking her with him and cradled her to his side, his warm skin heating her like a blanket.

"But?" He stiffened. "Are you having second thoughts? Regrets?"

"No!" She shook her head. "Not at all." She dropped and planted a kiss on his soft lips. "Never. It's just," she bit her lower lip, searching for the right words. "Our two worlds are so different. And I'm not supposed to know. Are we being realistic?"

"Whatever it takes. I'll do it. It won't be easy."

"We can fight together."

"You can't fight as a Guardian."

She smacked him in the chest. "Not that. For us. I'll fight for us."

He grasped her hand and brought her fingers to his mouth, kissing the tips. "Me too, baby. The Council knows about us."

She started to talk, but he stopped her with a shake of his golden head.

"I've taken care of it." His voice softened. "But this won't be easy. I'll be traveling a lot, whenever an assignment comes in."

"Same here. I'll be traveling for work."

"You'll see and hear some weird shit."

She laughed. "I'm sure, but I'm ready." She straddled him, grinding her hips against his groin, loving the groan that escaped his lips and the feral look he pierced her with. "There's no place I'd rather be, Gregor Magnuson. With you. Always with you."

EPILOGUE

One Year Later

KRISTA INHALED DEEPLY and looked at Gregor. His jaw locked in...what? Concentration? Concern? "You ready for this?"

They stood in front of a huge stone facade. The medieval castle looked ominous in the evening dusk. The gray stone battered by centuries of harsh Scottish weather and battles that Gregor had only touched upon as he began to explain the long history of the Magnuson family. The family had settled in Orkney centuries ago, part of a great Viking faction that had made their way over via the waterways.

When she'd first discovered that he was a gargoyle, she had some misgivings, even though she knew him to be a kind and gentle soul toward her. She'd had a few nightmares of him hovering above her in bed at night, his huge wings flapping loudly, disrupting the quietness of the night.

The scenario was implausible. Gregor did have wings, but he couldn't use them to fly and he'd shown them to her plenty since that day that seemed so long ago.

He held her hand tight in his, the muscle at his jaw working. She could see it pulsing. When he looked down at her and silently nodded, a wisp of nervousness crept up her spine. She knew it had been a long time since he'd been home. He'd wanted to come back for such a long time, but something always held him back.

She believed it all revolved around his relationship with his father. From what she'd learned, his father wasn't a huge supporter of his second-born son.

Even with his esteemed Guardian status.

Krista hadn't gotten the full story of what had happened to cause the friction between Gregor and the rest of his family, but she knew one day she'd hear about it. She just hoped now that he and Gunther had mended their relationship, that the same would be done with the rest of the family.

He and his mother had been close. He'd loved her dearly. Whenever he spoke about her his eyes and voice softened and took on a faraway look. Sadly, she'd passed years before and Krista had a feeling that her death may play a part in some of the friction between Gregor and his father.

The Guardian position played another. She didn't understand why he wasn't supportive of his son. But now that they were here, she was sure she before they left, she'd know the full story.

GREGOR LOOKED up at the pile of rocks he'd called home growing up. His memories were mixed - good and bad. Until his mother had passed, the good had outweighed the bad.

After she'd died, the formula reversed.

It had been decades since he'd been home. Perhaps more. He'd had no reason to come back. But he did. The second he and Krista stepped off the plane and out into the Scottish air, he'd breathed deep. A contentment that he didn't know he'd been missing seeped into his bones, welcoming him home.

He'd missed it. America was great and his work there had afforded him a wonderful life, but here, it was a whole different feeling.

The salty air livened him, awakening his senses to things he just couldn't get in the states. The fragrant scent of heather growing on the hills, the vibrant purple catching his eye as the unique fragrance tickled his nose. As they drove nearer to his ancestral home, Krista's hand in his, the swampy darkness of the moors reminded him of the years he and his siblings ran through them, chasing each other down.

He squeezed Krista's hand, and placed a soft kiss on her forehead. The love and support that shone in her eyes, was so much more than he deserved and he thanked the Gods every day for putting her in his path and allowing her to be a part of his life.

They walked slowly up the worn cobblestone path. Dread making his legs heavy, his feet drag.

How would his family accept him after all these years?

Would past issues come to the forefront?

The fact that after decades, his father had decided to host a family reunion was odd. Did he have an ulterior motive? He hoped not. When he'd first received the invite, he'd been tempted to ignore it. Why respond when he was almost certain his father didn't want him here in the first place?

But Gunther, being the mediator that he was, convinced him to come.

So, here he stood. The strongest woman he'd ever meant, supporting him at his side.

He grasped the metal handle of the gargoyle shaped knocker and banged it against the solid wood of the door three times and took a step back, waiting for someone to swing it open.

After what seemed liked ages, the door let out an ancient creak and swung open, and his father, who hadn't seen in over a century, stood in front of him. But instead of the stern look he was expecting, the one he'd remembered as a permanent fixture on his father's face, a warm smile greeted them. The elder Magnuson's eyes brightened as his gaze fell first on Gregor and then Krista.

"My son," he roared and grasped Gregor into a huge bear hug that he didn't know he longed for, but obviously wanted. "I'm glad ye could make it, lad. And yer lass, she's mighty bonny," he added before breaking the contact and focusing his attention on Krista.

"Good evening, Lass," he dipped his head and brushed a kiss on both of Krista's blushing cheeks. "I'm Vegard. So glad ye're here." He pumped her hand enthusiastically before letting it go. "Come in, come in. Everyone else is here."

The Great Room was alive with the love and laughter of his family. Everyone was there. Gunther had arrived yesterday. But his sisters and other brother, who he hadn't seen in almost as long as he'd last seen his father, were all seated at the family dining table. When he and Krista entered the room, they all stopped talking, growing silent for the few moments it took for them to register that he'd actually shown up.

And then it was like all Hell broke loose. They all stood, chair legs scraping loudly against the stone floors as they pushed back from the table and descended upon he and Krista so quickly, that for a few quick seconds he was worried for her safety. He'd not missed the widening of her beautiful brown eyes when they approached them, she looked so tiny compared to all of them, but she straightened her shoulders and met them all eye to eye, refusing to show that she may have been frightened. If his siblings noticed, they made no mention of it and embraced her warmly. Introducing themselves as they did.

He was positive, she'd have lots of questions for him later, but for now the information he'd given her about his family seemed to suffice.

This was not the welcome he'd expected. He questioned his memories. Maybe it was all in his head? Did he imagine the conflict between them all? His father looked at him with actual pride in his eyes.

The emotion was so unexpected, he was taken aback. He would've wagered his year's salary that his Da was angry that he'd been given the job of Dark Moor Guardian and not his older brother, who rightfully should have been first in line for the position.

But when he looked at his family now, all smiles, and love, there was nothing of the harsh words of the past.

They all took seats and passed around the ale and talked for hours. Catching up with everyone.

Later, with the midnight hour a distant memory, Gregor went outside for a breath of fresh air. He stood on one of the many balconies, looking over the murky darkness of the moors, the smell of moss strong in the air, when his father joined him.

"I can't tell you how much you coming home means to me, son." His father sighed. "I didn't think ye'd come."

Gregor sighed. "I wasn't going to."

His father nodded, his hair, just starting to gray at his temples, lifting in the breeze. "I understand."

They stood quietly, leaning on the balcony rail, their gazes roaming over the moors.

Several long moments passed. The only sound a pair of stoats fighting somewhere out in the dark landscape.

"As your brothers and sisters have come to visit over the years, there's always been a void in me heart."

Gregor remained silent. Waited for his father to continue.

"I know ye thought I was angry with ye, son. I wasn't. I was so proud of ye. Ye'd accomplished what I'd hoped for my sons."

Gregor went to say something, but his Da went on. "Throughout history, the Guardians have always been the first-born son. Ye broke that mold."

His jaw tensed, but he said nothing. He sensed this conversation was just as difficult for his father as it was for him.

"I'm sorry that ye felt I was disappointed in ye for gaining the position. I was," his father paused, "disappointed for Gunther. I knew how hard he worked for it. But, when I found out the reason Gunther lost was because the job went to ye? I was thrilled. But conflicted. How does a father show compassion and disappoint for one son and pride and excitement for another at the same time for the same job?"

Gregor shook his head. "I don't know." He pressed his lips into a thin line. And he didn't. He'd never realized the impossible position he and his brother had put their father in.

"Neither did I. Clearly, I handled it wrong. Because of that, we've had a fractured relationship, and I'm verra sorry for that."

He glanced at his father. The strong man who'd raised him and his siblings after their mother passed. The man who'd loved her with his whole being. So much so, that when his mother was alive, Gregor knew that their relationship was the type of relationship he wanted to have when he finally settled down.

He thought of the past. When he'd made The Guardians. The proudest moment of his life. He wanted nothing more to celebrate, yet, when he came home to tell his family, a somber vibe filled the air. Something he hadn't forgotten in all these years.

He felt guilty.

Selfish.

He was too blinded by his own ego to see how it affected his own family. Too blinded to see the position he put his father in.

Now he understood.

And he felt like an ass.

This rift was his fault. Due to his immaturity and refusing to see.

He sighed, a sigh he felt deep in his gut. At the same time, this invisible weight he'd carried around on his shoulders since he'd left home, lifted.

He clapped his father on the shoulder, and drew him into a hug that melted away years of fraught.

As they broke the hug, his Da's eyes were wet with unshed tears. Something he never expected to see from such a strong man.

"Da, I'm the one who needs to apologize. I think we Magnuson's need to really work on our communication skills. I see it now. I see how hard it was for you. Why I couldn't then, I don't know." He shrugged. "Maybe I refused to. I'm not sure, but I'm sorry. I'm sorry that we've lost all these years."

Vegard smiled, and waved his hand in the air. "That's all in the past. Let's promise to move forward. We've got many years in front of us to make it right." He gave a final glance to the moors before turning to go back inside. "I can feel your Mum's happiness shining down on us. Her family is once again whole. And growing!" He finished, referring to Krista.

Gregor reddened. He knew he couldn't trust Gunther to keep his mouth shut.

They entered the castle and Gregor stood back, watching his family. Watching Krista and Katla deep in conversation, their laughter, beautiful music to his ears. When Krista spotted him hanging back, she flashed him her dazzling smile, her love for him brightening her eyes.

He was the luckiest man on earth.

The luckiest gargoyle in the Otherworld.

Shoving his hands in his jeans pocket, his hand closed around the small box holding the ring he'd designed himself. It had been burning a hole in his pocket since he'd picked it up from the jeweler a month ago.

He hadn't known it when they arrived, but he'd found the perfect place to show Krista how much she meant to him.

Clearing his throat, he approached the chair where Krista sat and bent on one knee, some human customs were too good to pass up. Krista's eyes widened as he took her hand in his.

"Krista Wallingford, when I took on the assignment to protect you from a stalking skin walker, in the end, I never imagined it would be you doing the saving."

Her pale cheeks flushed and tears welled in her eyes. He reached into his pocket and pulled out the box and flipped it open, so Krista could see what it held.

"I know this year has opened your eyes to a whole new world. Will you let me continue to show you all the amazing things this world has to offer? Will you make me the luckiest being alive and marry me?"

Her free hand went to her mouth and covered a gasp. The tears that had formed were now freely running down her cheeks, leaving wet trails in their wake, as she nodded her head emphatically. "Yes!" She choked out on a happy sob before wrapping her arms around his neck, the force putting him off-balance and he fell back on his ass, she on top of him laughing and sobbing.

It was the perfect way to start the next chapter in their lives.

If you enjoyed *A Kiss of Stone*, please consider leaving a review at the retailer where you purchased this book to help the Dark Moor Guardians series grow.

***

Cover Design by Dar Albert, Wicked Smart Designs
Editing by Bethany Oliver

ALSO BY BRENNA ASH

Contemporary Romance
Pebble Harbor Series
Second Chances

ABOUT THE AUTHOR

Brenna Ash is addicted to coffee and chocolate. When she's not writing, she can be found either poolside reading a book, or in front of the TV, binge-watching her favorite shows, *Outlander* and *Sons of Anarchy*. She lives in Florida with her husband and a very, very spoiled cat named Lilly. She loves to interact with her readers on social media. Please feel free to follow her at the following platforms:

www.facebook.com/BrennaAshAuthor
www.twitter.com/brenna_ash
www.pinterest.com/ash0182
www.instagram.com/BrennaAshAuthor

To stay up to date on all things Brenna Ash, including book news, release dates and contest info, please sign-up for her newsletter on her website.

www.BrennaAsh.com

www.ingramcontent.com/pod-product-compliance
Lightning Source LLC
Chambersburg PA
CBHW011451170626
46816CB00009B/2623